He was there! I knew the instant I saw the big, black motorcycle that he was inside. The bike seemed enormous, like a great animal at rest. I felt thrilled just to look at it.

Katya punched my shoulder. "You'll probably get to ride on that thing, you lucky dog," she said.

"I doubt it," I told her, chaining my bike. "Just don't say anything to embarrass me, okay?"

She grinned. "What could I possibly say?"

Now my heart was really beginning to pound. Before this, I had felt cool — if Jason were there, fine. If not, fine. But now I knew he was really inside, that he might have come just to see me, and I didn't feel cool at all.

Other Point paperbacks
you will enjoy:

Acts of Love
by Maureen Daly

First a Dream
by Maureen Daly

No Promises
by Pamela Curtis Swallow

Sweetgrass
by Jan Hudson

point

HANDSOME AS ANYTHING

*Merrill
Joan Gerber*

SCHOLASTIC INC.
New York Toronto London Auckland Sydney

ISBN 0-590-43020-3

Copyright © 1990 by Merrill Joan Gerber.
All rights reserved. Published by Scholastic Inc.
POINT is a registered trademark of Scholastic Inc.

12 11 10 9 8 7 6 5 4 3 2 1   2   2 3 4 5 6 7/9

Printed in the U.S.A.   01

HANDSOME
AS ANYTHING

One

People disappoint me, which is why I have started wearing black. There isn't one person I know who doesn't have a fatal flaw — and that includes my mother and father; my two sisters, Franny and Erica; the male personage in my life, Rick (whom Mom calls my *little boyfriend* as in: "Is your *little boyfriend* coming around tonight?"); and all the counselors-in-training at Song of Solomon Day Camp, where I have a summer job taking care of little monsters.

Even Franny and Erica don't even seem like my sisters anymore, the way they throw insults at each other since Erica formally announced that she and

Harlan have set their wedding date for the last weekend in August.

Franny can't even be a good sport and offer congratulations — no, she rants and raves about the Big Mistake Erica is making. Ever since Franny went away to college at Berkeley and turned into a flaming feminist, she's totally against men and marriage. She trails after Mom, pointing out the errors of her ways in being so willing and anxious to serve Dad. She forgets that Mom has been acting this way with Dad forever, and it's no one's business but Mom's if she wants to cook his favorite things and iron his shirts — even the ones that don't need ironing.

No — no one acts his or her age. No one is kind or respectful; no one is even intelligent. In fact, I'm convinced everyone in my life is quite incredibly stupid . . . except maybe for Avram, the head counselor at Song of Solomon — but that's another story. If I so much as mentioned that I thought he was nice, Mom and Dad would want us to make it a double wedding with Erica and Harlan, which of course would be impossible, since Avram is a Yeshiva student studying to be a rabbi and would require a totally orthodox wedding. Whereas Harlan is Scotch/ex-Presbyterian — something totally friendly and vague — and he and Erica are planning some kind of creative ceremony in the woods, where they'll read poetry to each other they think is "significant," while everyone tosses gardenia petals at them.

This wedding plan is hard on everyone. Dad is crushed that Erica is not marrying a Jew (though

2

heaven knows he's not a big synagogue-goer), and Mom is crushed that Erica doesn't want a humongous wedding at some fancy hotel. Franny is just plain against weddings altogether; and I — well, I'm all for love and romance someday, but for me it seems about as far off as Mt. Kilimanjaro. In fact, I'd like to *be* on Mt. Kilimanjaro this minute, but I don't think this is a good time to ask my father to buy me mountain-climbing gear and lessons in mountaineering. He's still having a fit about all the money we spent on my aviary.

The truth is, everyone around me is just impossible, which is why I have to wear black. It's my reminder to myself that people are stupid, and there's just no hope for having a good time in this life. Dad stares at me when he sees my black clothes, and his eyebrows go half off his forehead — he probably thinks I'm going punk or heavy metal or something equally irrational (in his opinion). Anything that makes me more of an enigma to him just adds fuel to the fire in his brain. Almost daily he says to Mom, "See? It *has* to be from your side of the family! She takes after your crazy cousin Bertha. No one in *my* family ever acted the way Rachel acts."

Mom just wants to know why I've chosen such a dull, "monotone wardrobe." She's worried about what I'm going to do with all the fashionable shirts she's bought me. She's worried that I won't shop with her for a gown to wear to Erica's wedding. She's worried that I've misinterpreted her advice never to wear white or pastel pants: "One drop of chocolate ice cream, Rachel, one drop of spaghetti sauce, and that's the end of an expensive piece of clothing!"

I've told her she can just rest in peace now; I'm all done with expensive clothing. I can dress for a year on what I get from a few baby-sitting jobs if I shop at The Bargain Buggy. My mother calls it "the dead man's store," but actually it's the greatest place in the world. It's a thrift shop where shirts cost fifty cents (ten cents on sale days), and jeans or pants cost a dollar, and really magnificent coats, even down jackets and sailors' pea coats, cost only $2.50. On Stuff-Your-Bag day you can fill up a big paper bag for only $3! Where can you beat that?

I used to love going to Fashion Mall in my early innocent days, and it never bothered me to spend $22 for a shirt or a pair of pants, but now I would never set foot in a place like that. Franny took my fashion illusions apart once and for all when she explained that women like me spend money in malls just to dress up to please men. All that time I thought I had been buying pretty clothes to please myself. Now I don't really know *what* I think. If everyone left me alone for two seconds, I might figure it out.

But my mother is really nervous. She thinks I'm going to pick up leprosy from The Bargain Buggy. She always wants to fumigate me the instant I come back from shopping there. She screams, "Empty that bag right into the washer! Hurry up! God knows who wore those things. Do it right now!" Then she dumps a gallon of bleach into the machine and turns on water hot enough to boil someone alive in.

Of course I always put the washer on "Spin" and drain the water right out, clutching my bag of treasures against my chest. Bleach would *ruin* my black clothes, and the hot water would shrink my wonderful natural fibers — wool and cotton — down to nothing. I'd have to be a pygmy to get into those clothes by the time she got done with them.

Black is my banner these days. It's the color of my life. It's my statement. My daydreams have just the right contrast against black — I can look down at my shirt and see my future life painting itself: flaming reds of freedom and revolt; sweet, sad, dreamy violets and fuchsias of weeping and pain; and of course the ever present stroke, the stark cold ivory of loneliness.

Not every girl can make an art movie out of a black shirt, but that's what I do — I create myself this way and that way. Sometimes I see myself all together, and sometimes I see myself in pieces. Sometimes I'm a great beauty, and sometimes I'm just the real not-much-of-anything me: Rachel Leah Kaminsky, sixteen years old, smart for her age and going into twelfth grade a year ahead of herself because she skipped kindergarten, and spinning off in all directions like a crazy whirling dervish.

Two

"Let him kiss me with the kisses of his mouth —
For thy love is better than wine . . ."

Avram read the words, then looked across the circle of camp kids right into my eyes. I suddenly
remembered last night's dream, in which his lips
(coming toward me) were moist and pink inside
the dark forest of his beard. I suspected it wasn't
suitable for me to dream about a rabbinical student
that way, but no one ever told that to my subcon-
scious. I wondered if I ought to consider Avram,
who was twenty, an "older man." Was it because
he was a man or because he was older that he got

paid twice as much at camp as I did? I, a mere counselor-in-training, did twice as much work as he did. Well, when I was eighteen (if I still had this job) I would be a senior counselor, and some poor CIT would have to do all the work for *me*.

"Okay, kids," Avram said. "I just read you the first lines of the *Song of Solomon*. Since we take our camp name from that wonderful poem, we're each going to read our favorite parts of it today. You all have copies now — am I right? If you don't have a copy, raise your hand, and Rachel will give you one. Over there, Rachel; Danny doesn't have one."

Danny, wearing his dumb Woody Woodpecker shirt, started waving his hands in the air. He was our resident troublemaker who probably had a genius IQ, but his purpose in life was to drive everyone crazy.

"I don't want to read this stuff," Danny said. "I want to work on my lanyard."

"We aren't doing lanyards yet," I said. "This isn't lanyard day. It's *Song-of-Solomon* day."

"Listen to this — it's the stupidest thing I ever read: 'Your hair is like goats. Your nose is like a tower. . . .'"

"It's great poetry, Danny," Avram said in his deep, melodious voice. "It doesn't mean literally what it says, it comes to its meaning obliquely."

"Any way you come to goats, they stink," Danny said. "And anyone who has a nose like a tower ought to have plastic surgery. My mother did when she was nineteen. She had a nose like — "

"Never mind," I said, cutting him off. If I were Danny's mother, I wouldn't want my son giving away my secrets. "Either find a part you like or just listen quietly while the others read theirs."

Avram nodded approvingly at the way I was handling this. I felt myself flush with pleasure. At first I'd been disappointed to have the kids who were ten and eleven. I had been hoping for the six- and seven-year-olds, who were cute and malleable, but when I found out Avram would be working with my group, I figured I could put up with the older ones.

I thought I might be beginning to fall in love with him. Here, I reasoned, was a serious person, not like all the stupid people I knew, but a person who meditated on the meaning of life. A man who thought about Big Things like God (I wasn't too sure about God myself) and Ethics and Decency. Compared to my "little boyfriend" Rick, who mainly thought about getting a better bass sound out of his speakers, Avram was what my father called a *mensch*, a solid, real, complete human being. If I fell in love with Avram, at last I would have one interest of which my father might finally approve! A Jewish boy! My father had made it clear to me since I was about ten days old that he expected me to marry a Jewish boy. I didn't think that was fair because his main answer to my questions about *why* he wanted me to marry a Jew was: "Because we're Jews and that's that." I don't know what happened with Erica, since she was ending up with a Scotch/ex-Presbyterian, but I figured it was safer not to ask him.

Avram cleared his throat and began to read to the kids:

*"How beautiful are thy steps in sandals,
    O prince's daughter . . ."*

Avram went on about the beloved's navel being a goblet and her belly a heap of wheat. When he came to *"Thy two breasts are like two fawns that are twins of a gazelle . . ."* Danny hooted.

"I saw a gazelle on *Wild Kingdom*," Danny said. "What do breasts have to do with gazelles?" he guffawed. I wanted to whap him on the head and tell him he had a brain like a hyena. I wanted to kill him for interrupting. I desperately wanted all the kids to disappear, so Avram and I could read this love poem to each other.

Could it be he read my mind? Because he said, "You and I will have to continue this another time, Rachel. Preferably just the two of us."

Then he dismissed the kids to go to the crafts room.

"Really?" I said. "Just the two of us?" I was hoping we could execute his plan that very minute.

But then he said, his voice purely business, "I trust you're all ready for the camp-out tonight?"

"God! Did you have to remind me? Fifteen monsters at Fulton Flats! I'll never survive." Then I was sorry I had said "God" so lightly, because Avram's eyebrows went up and his forehead seemed to pucker. I didn't like his face when he frowned; it had a hard look. "Will you be going with us?" I asked him. I already knew the answer.

"Afraid not, Rachel," he said. "I'm not scheduled for camp-outs. I'll be studying. But of course the other counselors will be there."

"Of course," I said.

"And they have a full agenda of activities planned for the kids. It ought to go well."

"It ought to," I said.

"I hope you have a good experience."

"Thank you, Avram," I said. "I sincerely hope so, too."

Three

"Aah — Rachel Leah Kaminsky," my father greeted me on Friday afternoon as I came stumbling in the front door with my backpack, my duffel, and my sleeping bag. "How nice that you're home from your camp-out. Now you can help me carry the garbage pails around to the front."

I should have known better, but for a minute my heart actually lifted when he said, "How nice that you're home." I'd forgotten in my one night's absence from home that the main use my father has for me is as the person on the other side of the garbage can.

You'd think my father had gone to school all

those years to get his Ph.D. in Garbage Disposal instead of in Political Science. He seems to have this obsessive compulsion to pare down, trim away, and clean up. Every summer he spends hours each day clipping perfectly healthy leaves off trees and bushes and ivy till nothing is left but naked little bumpy branches, and then he packs them all into garbage cans, stamping down on them to pack them even tighter, and then he asks me to help him carry the cans out front.

Whenever I hear him calling my name, my *full* name (like now), I just know what's in store for me. Never a little father-daughter talk about how I'm doing in school, or when we can schedule a date for my driver's test, or what I want to be when I grow up (thank God for that!), but only another garbage trip.

"Just give me one second, Dad," I told him. "I need to go to the bathroom." While I was in there, I pictured the usual encounter between Dad and me. This is how it goes: We take a long trek around the side of the house, each of us holding a handle on this ten-ton garbage can, always out of step; my father tends to jerk the can and nearly dislocates my shoulder while the plastic handle cuts into my hand — and then, when we pass the aviary, he always says exactly the same thing. "Well, Rachel, we built this fancy aviary for you, but you don't seem too interested in your birds anymore. It's really a pity, isn't it? I thought you were going to be an ornithologist."

My father says this every time we pass the cage,

rain or shine, winter or summer. Sometimes he adds, "That chicken wire was really expensive — we thought it would be a lifelong interest of yours, your mother and I."

"I still like birds," I usually mumble. What does he know of my tragedies with my birds? Did *he* ever sit outside all night to make sure the father finch didn't pull tufts of feathers out of the nestlings' heads to feather the nest with them? Did *he* ever keep a vigil to see the baby button quails hatch their way out with the little drills of their egg teeth? I'm sure my father, Melvin Kaminsky, Ph.D., would never in a thousand years have the patience to sit in front of the aviary and record (as I did) the eating, mating, singing, and sleeping habits of my two waxbills.

What could he possibly know of my devotion and of my grief? When a heat wave killed the baby birds, and I found them dead, with ants crawling in their eyes — did *he* cry? And when a raccoon picked open the lock and got my two mourning doves (didn't even eat them, just killed them!), did *my father* bury them under the apricot tree? All he knows is that he spent money for the chicken wire!

That's how parents are. They're willing to spend money on you if they're sure it will give you an educational advantage. If they buy you a toy doctor kit, they want you to swear on your life you'll be a brain surgeon; if they buy you a plastic whistle, they want you to be a flutist like James Galway; and if they buy you a parakeet, you've got to turn into a bird genius like Audubon. My father forgets that he has a clarinet tucked up in the closet; that he bought an exercycle he never uses; that the pieces of his carved mahogany chess set sit on their chessboard like so many embalmed mummies.

"I'm waiting for you, Rachel Leah Kaminsky," my father called through the bathroom door.

"Daddy," I said, coming out, shaking twigs from my hair. "Do you know I have just been at Fulton Flats overnight with fifteen wild kids? Do you know I am sunburned, exhausted, and practically have a skull fracture from when a bunk fell on my head?"

"It will only take a minute, Rachel Leah," he said. He looked like a cartoon character in his striped T-shirt and his plaid walking shorts.

"I have a headache," I said. "I want to take a shower."

"It's best to shower after you handle garbage," he said, reasonably. "I've been waiting all day for you to come home so we could do this together."

"That's really nice," I said.

He smiled. He thought I really meant it. You can't be sarcastic with him; he's too innocent.

"You could ask Franny," I said. "Couldn't you?"

"You know I can't," my father said. "Franny is sick."

"Oh, yes," I said. "I do recall that fact."

He smiled again because he was sure we both wanted Franny's total recovery from mononucleosis, which she conveniently picked up at college. Franny had him completely intimidated (more power to her!). He knew he couldn't con her into the garbage detail. Not when her main mission in life was to see that men would never "walk all over her."

Sometimes I wonder where Franny got the courage to stop shaving her legs and underarms, to give up makeup and high heels, and never to wear what she calls "sexed clothes," but she got it *somewhere*. Maybe it means I have some courageous genes, too.

"Follow me," said Dad, a leader of men.

So I followed him into the backyard. When Basil and Itzhak saw him, they took off into the high grass to hide. My father has never petted a single furry creature in his life, and my cats know that instinctively. They get out of his way, fast.

Dad had clipped the oleander bushes this time. They looked positively ravished. "What happened to all the flowers?" I asked as I picked up my side of the garbage pail.

"Those flowers are poisonous, Rachel," my father said. "They have to be kept under control; they have to know who's boss."

"I guess a corsage of them could sneak into the house and attack us some night," I said.

"Not only that . . ." my father said, jerking his end of the can so that I had to leap after him, ". . . if there were ever a fire, and all those leaves burned, we could die from inhaling the smoke."

"You could install a fire alarm in the backyard somewhere," I suggested.

"I never thought of that." He looked at me with approval. "Rachel," he said, "you're a very bright girl, but there are times I think that you might not take the right path in life."

"*Is* there a right path? And if there is, are you sure you know what it is?" (Those had to be my courageous genes talking.)

"Well, I've been thinking about something very important, and I want to talk to you about it."

"Now? Here in the alley?" I asked.

"Yes."

"Then could we please put down the garbage pail?"

"Oh. Well, of course."

We stood there, with the poisonous oleanders between us.

"Rachel, I feel I have failed you."

"In what way, Daddy?"

"Your mother and I have not given you a serious Jewish education."

"I don't mind," I said. "I don't feel like being a *serious* Jew. I mean, you don't have to worry. I know I'm a Jew. I know some Jewish history and all that. I could even recite the *Song of Solomon* to you right now, if you wanted me to."

"I'll tell you what worries your mother and me," my father said.

"It's Erica's boyfriend, right? I mean, you wish he were Jewish."

"He's a fine young man," my father said. "But . . . my grandchildren," Dad said.

"They'll be Jewish, don't worry. Any baby born of a Jewish mother is Jewish. Even mine will be. It's the law."

"I trust you're not going to make me a grandfather for a while," my father said. "But I do wish you would want to take your religion more seri-

16

ously, so that when you choose a mate, you will consider the importance of similar values and backgrounds."

"Did you discuss all this with Franny, too?"

"Franny has made it clear to us that she's beyond all traditional matters of sex and religion. You, luckily, are still approachable." He smiled at me in that sweet way he has. But I was thinking of something else he had said.

Matters of sex. A vision of Avram's beard popped into my head like magic. Almost without thinking I said to my father, "Well, Daddy, you'll be glad to know I've made a new friend at camp — he's definitely Jewish. In fact, he's going to be a rabbi!"

"Really? Why didn't you say so?" Suddenly my father leaned over the garbage can and kissed me on my forehead. "I'm so pleased, Rachel. I can't tell you how relieved I am."

"This doesn't mean I'm getting married to him yet, or anything," I cautioned him. "I mean, all he and I do is make lanyards together."

"It's a start," my father said. "Yes, indeed. A start in the right direction. Erica's Harlan is a fine boy, but what does he know about the great past of the Jews, of Jewish history?"

(How much do *you* know? I thought, but I didn't ask him. My father has probably not been in a synagogue since his wedding, although my mother regularly pays the yearly dues of our Jewish congregation, and often goes to the book review group sponsored by the Sisterhood. She *always* goes to the Las Vegas night fund-raiser.)

My father continued to seem unusually pleased

17

with me. "A Jewish boyfriend," he mused. "Good." Then we lifted the garbage can and went jerking along down the alley. We passed the aviary. Fudgy, my widowed finch, stared at us from his perch and sang his sad, funereal song.

"Well, Rachel," my father said. "We built this fancy aviary for you but you don't seem too interested in your birds anymore. It's really a pity, isn't it? I thought you were going to be an ornithologist."

"I'm thinking now maybe I should be an orthodox lady-rabbi, Daddy."

He actually thought I was serious. He said, "But you would definitely need to learn Hebrew first, Rachel . . . and maybe after you graduate from high school your mother and I can figure out a way to send you to Israel."

"There's no need to worry about that, yet, Daddy," I assured him. We clunked the garbage can down on the curb.

"Only three more cans to go," Dad said cheerfully. "Then you can pop into the shower."

Four

"Are you going out with your little boyfriend this afternoon?" Mom asked me in the morning as I was having breakfast. She was rehanging the curtains over the kitchen sink and fluffing out their ruffles.

"I guess," I mumbled. I was eating mashed avocado and natural peanut butter on cracked wheat bread with a pickle on the side — Franny's daily breakfast since she'd adopted an entirely new and radical view about nutrition as a result of living in her co-op in Berkeley. To please her, my mother had completely ceased cooking those old and ruinous standbys: pancakes dripping with butter,

French toast fried in oil, or eggs, any style, bursting with cholesterol.

"We can always tell when you're going out," Franny said. "You always wear your favorite black shirt, the one with three holes in the front." Franny took a bite of a sour pickle, and a scent of garlic wafted toward me.

"Oh, look what *you* wear all the time," I said. "You shouldn't talk!" Franny had worn the same exact outfit since the day she'd come home for summer vacation — a purple tie-dyed shirt and shredded purple shorts. She'd had a job lined up for the summer ever since spring vacation, in the mall at 31 Flavors, scooping ice cream, but then she came down with mono and had a totally right-eous excuse to lounge around and read, with everyone serving her and putting pillows under her poor ravaged body. Right now she was reading *Toward a More Radical Feminism*. Yesterday it had been *The Second Sex* by Simone de Beauvoir.

"You know I love your black shirt," Franny said, lifting a handful of alfalfa sprouts from the plastic container and chewing them delicately. "You know I approve of everything you're doing these days."

"Yes," Mom said coldly. "The more Rachel be-comes like you, and the worse she dresses, the more you approve of her."

"Why not?" Franny asked airily. "She's my flesh and blood. Haven't you always told us there are no people on earth closer than sisters? They share the same exact parents, the same home, the same genetic heritage — it's nearly miraculous. So why shouldn't I take an active interest in Rachel's development? She's practically *me!*"

"You're only teaching her to be as antisocial as you are!" Mom said.

"Me? Antisocial?" Franny asked. She looked up and smiled at Mom. "I have *loads* of friends, Mother. You can hardly deny that."

"I can hardly deny that," Mom agreed, smoothing her flowered apron. "But your girlfriends and boyfriends all look alike. I can hardly tell them apart when they drop over here. The girls don't wear any makeup. Some of the boys wear earrings! The girls have short hair, the boys have long hair."

"Long hair is nothing new," Franny said. "It's been around since the sixties."

"I didn't care much for the sixties," Mom said.

"It sometimes seems to me you didn't even *notice* them," Franny said. "*Did* you?"

"I was busy making a home," Mom said, "if that's what you mean. I wasn't out marching in political protests or sending letters to my congressmen."

"But didn't *any* of it filter through?" Franny got up from the kitchen table and went over to hug Mom. It was funny — how she could argue and at the same time be affectionate and loving.

Mom accepted her hug. It was hard for anyone to be angry with Franny for long; she was so sweet and beautiful. It didn't matter that she dressed in rags — no one ever noticed them, overshadowed as they were by the radiance of her smile, by her expressive dark eyes, and by the natural grace of her form. She was a feminist who was so intrinsically feminine that no amount of "unsexed" clothing could conceal that she was a beautiful woman. Her hair was her one indulgence: She never cut it. She loved it as she loved any necessary, functioning part of her body. She washed it every day and was always tossing her head this way and that to encourage it to dry. It's probably never really been totally dry, except maybe on some summer day when it gets to 100 degrees, or when she's been in the sun at the beach for ten hours.

Mom gave in and hugged Franny back. "Oh, you dopey girl," she said, laughing and trying to look disapproving at the same time. "I don't want you teaching all your funny ideas to Rachel. She could use a little makeup, you know. She could use a little better taste in clothes."

What Mom really meant was that I couldn't get by, like Franny, on being naturally beautiful. If I let myself go (as she obviously thought I was doing) there wouldn't be a chance for me at all, not in the world Mom lived in. I'd probably be an old maid.

But that was the whole problem! Everyone's worlds! The world Franny lived in! Avram's world! My father's world! Erica's world! None of them was my world! *Where was I going to find my world?*

My mother had a strange look on her face. I had a feeling she was about to launch into a speech about my room being a mess, or that I'd better get busy powdering the cats before we all caught typhus from fleas they'd picked up in the yard. But she said, "Daddy told me you met a rabbinical student at camp, Rachel. We're very pleased he's your new friend."

"What's this all about?" Franny asked at once.

"It's nothing," I said. "Don't make a big thing of it. He's just this guy I know at day camp."

"He's going to be a rabbi?"

"So he says." Now I wished I hadn't said a word. It was amazing what people could do with one tiny bit of information.

"Let me just warn you," Franny said. "The wives of orthodox rabbis stay home and make noodle pudding while the men do the really important stuff of talking to God and keeping the world going."

"Hey! I'm not his wife!" I said. "I'm merely his partner in arts and crafts!"

"What are you thinking?" Franny demanded of me. "You have to be nuts if you're thinking of falling in love with a rabbi! I can't believe this household. Erica getting married at barely twenty-one; you going to stay home and light sabbath candles all your life. Ritual and subjugation. What's going on?"

Her question made me think of Avram's dark sexy beard, of his singing, melodious rabbi-type voice, of his dark eyes. I was thinking of the words of the *Song of Solomon*, and of how Avram and I might read it together — alone — eventually.

"Don't be mad at me," Franny said suddenly. "I have only your interests at heart."

"So does everyone," I said. "That's the problem."

Franny poked her finger in a hole in my black shirt. "Gee, I wish I had a shirt like this one," she said. "It's classy."

"You can come with me the next time Katya and I go to The Bargain Buggy. Maybe you'll find one just like it there."

"I can't go out in the world. I'm already dying of mono," she said. "Who knows what else I would come home with from that place!"

"You sound just like Mom!" I accused her.

"A fate worse than death!" she said. Then she hugged me. I hugged her back. I couldn't help it. You just have to love Franny.

Five

Franny and I loaded the dishwasher together, and then she said, "Come to my room for a minute." I followed her down the hall and glanced into my sister Erica's room — she was out with Harlan for the day. Her favorite six-foot-high Saint Bernard stuffed animal sat at the foot of her bed with his little wooden barrel strapped around his neck. Harlan was also six feet tall, and fuzzy, too, like a huggy bear, with curly brown hair and lots of hair on his arms and chest. I wondered if Erica was just exchanging one stuffed animal for another. She still had her high school banner on her wall, and bride dolls of many countries on her shelf, and a paperweight she had made in Girl Scouts on her desk.

A shiver went through me when I thought of the room without her by the end of the summer: my sister Erica — *A Married Woman.*

We passed the little storage closet I used for my darkroom. My father had indulged me in that, too, as well as in the aviary. He had bought me a used enlarger, a 35-millimeter camera, plastic developing trays, a timer, a drying rack — and of course he was annoyed that I hadn't become Ansel Adams yet, either.

"Too bad you don't use the darkroom very much," Franny said. "You used to be so interested in all that stuff."

"Yeah, I know," I said. I would have thought she'd be more sensitive. But in a way, she was like the rest of the adults; she *was* an adult, eighteen, and she was beginning to talk as if she saw certain things from their point of view.

"I was hoping to use it a lot this summer, but the thing is, I have to use it after dark, and Mom and Daddy go to bed so early! If I run the water in the bathroom after ten or eleven at night, which is when I have to wash my negatives, they have a fit. 'You're keeping us up; don't you know we need to get our rest?' You'd think they were ninety-five, the amount of sleep they seem to need."

"Old people need very little sleep, as a point of fact," Franny said, leading me into her room, stepping over piles of books she had strewn all over the floor. "Sit down," she said, throwing a handful of purple shirts off her desk chair.

I sat down.

"Don't sit like that," Franny said.

"How is that?" I looked down. I was sitting like a regular person, my behind on the chair, my feet on the floor, my hands crossed in my lap.

"Don't sit like a girl."

"What should I sit like, a gorilla?"

"That would certainly be better," Franny said. "I never thought to call up that image, but a gorilla would be fine. Sort of hanging all over the place."

"What *are* you talking about?"

"I'm reading this book — " Franny said. She waved an orange book at me. "It's about body language."

I crossed my legs.

"There! You're doing it!" She pointed an accusing finger at me. "You're drawing yourself in. You just crossed your legs. That's what the subordinate group always does. Women are afraid to take up space. Think about it, Rachel. Think how women sit. They sit with their legs crossed and their hands in their laps. And how do *men* sit? Men are the dominant group in this society, right? They *sprawl*, they *fling*. They *stretch*. They stick their legs way out, and they crash their arms about over the backs of couches, and they swing chairs around and straddle them, and they take over all the territory within reach!"

She smiled at me, raising her finely shaped, naturally thick eyebrows. "I learned all this in my Women's Studies class. And see? See what I mean? Look at you, sitting there like a little compressed lump: elbows in, legs crossed shyly, so feminine, so virginal."

"Funny you can get so much out of my just sitting down on your chair."

"I just needed to make my point," Franny said. "You're young, you have a lot to learn. I feel responsible for educating you."

I heard my name being called from the kitchen.

"That's Daddy," I said. "I think he's just filled up another garbage pail."

"You mustn't let him control you," Franny said.

"I don't," I said. "I just help him with the garbage. It's the least I can do in return for his supporting me all these years."

"Men are always supporting women!" Franny said. "And we always feel indebted. That's the trouble!"

"Would you like to carry my half of the garbage can?" I asked. "He's been supporting you, too."

"I have mono," Franny said. "I'm sorry, but I can't."

In the kitchen my father was getting a drink of water. He was holding his clipping shears under one arm.

"I need some help outside with the cans, Rachel Leah," he said. "But first I need to sit down and rest a minute. Want a drink?"

"No thanks, Dad," I said. I pulled out a kitchen chair and swung it around, crashing it into the cabinet. I straddled it, spreading my legs and letting my feet flail wildly. I accidentally kicked my father in the shins. I swung my arms backward and knocked a glass off the counter. I wasn't going to be a compressed lump the rest of my life.

"What's the matter?" my father said, looking alarmed. "Are you having a fit or something? I remember you said a bunk fell on your head at the camp-out."

"It's okay, Daddy," I said. "Don't worry. I'm just doing what Franny taught me. I'm taking up the space I deserve."

Six

I was reading *Our Schoolroom Is on the Mountain*, a book put out by The Mountainside School, this amazing place that takes kids into the wilds of America for their senior year of high school. The students who are accepted live on a bus and study the greatest stuff imaginable: wildlife, birds, stars, and rocks. They camp out, travel across the country, rough it, and get to live in nature. It all sounded very attractive to me except for the part about "personal relationships." I read that part a second time to be sure I understood it:

One of our requirements is that young people who are accepted into our program are not permitted to "pair off" during the year, since relationships of this sort, which develop in a small, confined group, tend to lead toward cliquishness and feelings of jealousy and distress in other members of the group.

I decided that — interesting as the program seemed — I probably wouldn't apply for admission (the deadline was midsummer) because I'd never want to be in a school situation where there was a rule against falling in love.

Just then there was a knock on my bedroom door. This always posed a dilemma for me. If I said, "Yes?" and it was my father or mother knocking, he (or she) would immediately open my door and stick his (or her) head in. Nothing I might say was ever a signal for them *not* to open my door. Only Franny and Erica had the good sense to answer my "Yes?" with the proper question: "May I come in?"

Now I tried a new tack. "Just a minute, please," I said — and waited, holding my breath. If I said, "I'm getting dressed," and it turned out to be my mother knocking, she would push open the door and say, "It's only your mother," as if mothers had total and permanent rights to intrude on one's privacy for one's entire life.

Now I heard silence. Was my mother gone? Or was she going to wait the literal "one minute" I'd asked for before she barged in? Suddenly the door swung open. A column of laundry marched in.

"The least you could have done was open it

31

for me," she complained, her voice muffled, her face hidden. "Of course you didn't get to folding the laundry as I asked you to, so I had to do it myself. . . ." She paused for effect. "Here it is, all clean and folded for the convenience of Your Highness."

"Thanks, Mom," I said, "but you didn't have to go and do it yourself. I told you I'd get to it as soon as I could."

"I can't wait that long," she said. "I am not likely to live to be two hundred. I only have a normal life span to look forward to."

"Mom — " I said, "do you mind if I ask you why you bother to knock on my door if you're going to walk right in anyway?"

"Why, it's *polite* to knock," my mother said, going directly to my dresser and tucking my underpants in one drawer, my socks in another. She opened my top drawer and then paused, puzzled. "How come I have no clean bras of yours here to put away?" she asked. "Did you forget to put them in the wash?"

"I'm not wearing bras anymore."

"Why not? You need to wear a bra, Rachel. You'll get all sagged out of shape if you don't. Has Franny put some radical idea into your head about this?"

"Well, Franny pointed out that bras focus attention on *parts*, and women aren't made of *parts*."

"Just a couple of months ago I bought you some perfectly nice bras," my mother said, ignoring what I had just told her, poking about in the drawer. "If

I'm not mistaken, we spent a good deal of money for them."

"Bras feel tight," I said. "They bother me. How come men, but not women, are allowed to wear nice loose things all the time?"

"Men don't have breasts," my mother said simply.

"Well, they have *feet*, don't they? And they don't have to wear high heels. And they don't have to wear short dresses that make it impossible for them to move without being conscious of their underpants being exposed. . . ."

"Rachel," my mother said. "You don't want to go out into the world *jiggling*, do you?"

"I can't see what's so awful about that."

"Well, bras not only support you," she added. "They cover up the *outlines* of certain critical parts of your body. You don't want people looking through your clothes."

"I wear black," I reminded her. "No one can look through black unless he has X-ray vision."

"Black is for a funeral," my mother said.

"Well, maybe there'll be a funeral coming up soon," I said. I couldn't help myself.

"Death is *not* a matter for a joke," my mother said. "Your father could drop dead of a heart attack any day, working out in the sun, pruning and mowing and clipping as if he needs to store up hay for the winter!"

"No one makes him do it," I said. I wanted to get back to reading *Our Schoolroom Is on the Mountain*. In fact, under the circumstances, The Mountainside School suddenly seemed extremely attractive to me, falling in love allowed or not. I definitely might want to live in a bus for a year in order to get very far away from here. I decided I would write away for an application at once and apply for admission, just in case. I realized that I needed some insurance to allow me to escape from home next year! College was too long to wait.

"Oh — I forgot to tell you," Mom said. "Your little friend Rick is here. He's outside, waiting under the orange tree. I asked him to come in, but he said he didn't want to leave his moped unattended in the yard. Daddy was out there pulling weeds; he offered to watch it, but your friend said he couldn't trust it with *anyone*."

"Well, that's Rick, all right. Thanks for the message, Mom. And would you please leave my room now? And do you think I might be able to put a lock on my door some day?"

"What for?" she said. "Do you have something to hide?"

Rick was perched on his moped under the orange tree, wearing his crash helmet with built-in stereo earphones. His Walkman radio was clipped to his belt beside his solar calculator. I could see — sticking out from the saddle bag — a bunch of new videos he had rented for his VCR. He was so busy adjusting the equalizer in his crash helmet that I finally had to knock on the fiberglass dome of it to get his attention.

"Oh, hi," he said.

We both glanced down toward my father, who

had just finished weeding around the base of the succulents and was headed across the grass toward the orange tree, sliding on his rear end over the few feet he had to traverse.

"Here comes the human mower," I said. "Watch out."

"Want to see the new movies I got?" Rick asked.

"I guess," I said. I had so many things I'd rather do: work in the darkroom, read some more about The Mountainside School, memorize the *Song of Solomon* to impress Avram. Rick began to pull out tape after tape. I sort of got the impression right away: *The Blob*, *Jaws III*, *Rocky IV*, *Superman V*.

"Want to come over to my house and watch them with me? Or we could watch them in your house."

"No, thanks," I said. I was reading the description on *The Blob* tape: *An oozing mass of carnivorous gelatin devours a small town*. "Why don't we just sit in the backyard and talk or something?"

"Or how about we go to Blast-Off Arcade in the mall and play video games?"

"I'd rather just talk."

"Talk?" Rick looked baffled, as if he had no idea what I meant. I knew our days of friendship were numbered. In fact, I decided they were over as of today. I had broached the subject of talk many times before. His eyes always rolled up into his head. I don't know why I had let him keep coming around. I suppose I thought I needed some kind of male personage to verify that I was female. But now there was a better one in my life: Avram.

"Excuse me," my father said. He was having a

hard time with a stubborn, giant weed.

"Rick," I said. "Why don't you go home and play chess with your computer game?"

"How come?"

"Because I just remembered I have to study," I said.

"School's out," he said. "No one studies when school's out."

"I do," I said. "I'm a weird person, Rick. And I'm getting weirder all the time."

"Yeah, maybe you are." He shrugged.

"So — so long," I said. "I gotta go. Invitations greater than *The Blob* are calling out to me."

"Okay," he said. He revved up his motor. He didn't seem to be dying of grief. "See you," he said. He waved and roared off.

"Nice boy," my father said. "But not Jewish," he added, as if I didn't know.

"Don't worry, Daddy," I said. "We've just called off our betrothal."

Seven

When the camp bus picked me up on Monday and headed off toward Song of Solomon Day Camp, I started humming a song from *Fiddler on the Roof*:

> *"For Papa, make him a scholar,*
> *For Mama, make him a rich as a king,*
> *For me, well, I wouldn't holler*
> *If he were as handsome as anything!"*

I had loved the movie of *Fiddler on the Roof* right up to the moment Tevye disowns one of his five wonderful daughters in the "Never darken my doorstep again" scene. That's when the daughter decides to marry a perfectly good, kind, decent young man, who just happens to be a Russian peasant and a non-Jew. It made me feel sick that Tevye, such a good father in other ways, would consider his daughter "dead" to him because she fell in love with a non-Jew. Weren't parents always trying to raise their children to be fair and not bigoted and to judge each person as an individual? Then — boom. Suddenly perfectly nice parents threatened never to love you again unless you did what they wanted. I hoped I wouldn't be that kind of parent someday. I hoped I could hang onto my principles!

As we pulled into the synagogue parking lot, my heart jumped when I saw Avram standing there, meeting the bus as he did every morning, wearing his black trousers and white shirt, shading his eyes as the bus driver parked, and the kids began to spill out. Yes, Avram really was definitely "handsome as anything." For Papa, he *was* a scholar. For Mama, well, he probably wasn't rich as a king yet, but maybe he would be. And for me, well, I wasn't going to holler. No indeed, not with that beard to look at, those intense, intelligent eyes, that tall, nicely formed body. I got off the bus and, coming down the step, pretended to lose my balance slightly (a trick Franny would hate me for!). But it worked. Avram jumped forward and put out his hand to steady me. The thing is, he didn't quite touch me. He just *almost* did.

"I'll give you a rundown of our schedule for today, Rachel," he said. "Hebrew folk songs on the patio, and then origami in the crafts room. And you — the expert — get to lead the origami session."

"Oh, not me! I don't know *anything* about origami, Avram," I said.

"But it's right here in your camp application." He tapped a black looseleaf notebook he held under his arm. "It says in your application that you can do soap carving, make puppets, lead folk dancing, sing Yiddish songs, and do origami. If I'm not mistaken, you can also bake *challah* and take kids on bird walks and teach animal behavior."

"Bird walks! I can do that. But as for all that other stuff, it's all made up."

"Who made it up?

"It must have been my mother."

"*Your mother?* Who filled out your camp application form?"

"Well, she did. I didn't know it at the time. She wanted me to have a summer job, so when she saw the ad for a CIT in the temple newsletter, she got an application from the office and filled it out for me. She knows I'm not so good at (as she calls it) 'blowing my own horn.' Besides, she probably thinks I *can* do all those things."

"That wasn't a very upright or honorable thing for her to do," Avram said, frowning. "I was counting on you to lead the group today."

"You can still count on me, Avram. I'll play it by ear. I'll read the directions on the origami box. And I'll brush up on that other stuff in the library. And tonight I'll try to get some pointers on baking *challah*. My friend Katya Ohlendorf's grandfather used to be a baker in Germany, and her brother, Karl, goes to some famous bakers' college in Chicago, except he's home for the summer now. *Someone* in that family can probably teach me to bake a *challah*."

"You have a German friend?" Avram asked. We were at the entrance to the synagogue, and he came to stand beside a pillar that I was leaning against. He pressed his palm against the pillar and bent toward me. I had noticed, ever since Franny had pointed it out to me, how often men did that — how they leaned over women. Franny said it was an instinct for domination. Probably unconscious, but maybe not. Actually, I liked the feeling of his leaning over me, though I would never admit that to Franny.

"Yes — Katya's my best friend, except maybe for my sister Franny," I said. "Katya Ohlendorf is her name. She and I bike to The Bargain Buggy every Saturday — that's a thrift shop where we love to shop. It's the cheapest store in town. My mother calls it 'the dead man's store.' "

"You say she's German?"

"Who?" I had suddenly lost the train of conversation as I watched Avram's eyes, the curl of his beard.

"Your friend Katya is German?"

"She's American, I guess," I said. "Like the rest of us in America."

"But originally."

"Her parents are from Germany, yes."

"Parents? Or grandparents?"

"Parents," I said. "They came over after the war. They had Katya late in life. And her brother, Karl, too. He's older — he's the baker."

"You know this brother . . . . Karl?" He said the name as if he had a hair on his tongue.

"Sort of, I mean — he's usually around when I go over there. I just met him a week or so ago." I was feeling a little closed-in by Avram's arm. "Listen — the kids are probably in the crafts room throwing ten thousand Popsicle sticks on the floor. Don't you think we ought to go in?"

"Rachel," Avram said. He took a step closer to me and lowered his head to stare into my eyes. "I think you ought to reconsider having a best friend who is *German*. Since the war, most serious Jews would never even consider such a thing."

"I don't get it," I said. His expression worried me.

"German," Avram repeated. "*Germany. War. Hitler.*"

"Oh, that," I said. "I don't believe in holding grudges forever. Katya and I are buddies. We aren't at war with each other."

"But her father — he may have been in Hitler's army."

"No — he wasn't. Katya told me he wasn't in the war."

"That's not the point," Avram said. "Maybe he saluted Hitler when Hitler marched past. Maybe he had friends who were Nazis."

"Maybe he did, maybe he didn't, but so what? Katya isn't saluting anyone. Katya isn't a Nazi."

41

"The *point*," he said, giving his foot a little stamp for emphasis, "is that Germans and Jews can never be friends."

"Why not?" I insisted.

"You know why," Avram said. "Don't tell me you don't know about the death camps."

"Of course I know," I said. "But do you think the members of every German and Jewish generation from now on should hate one another?"

"Perhaps it's necessary," Avram said. "Yes, I think the answer is yes. Try to imagine what it would have been like to have lost a mother or father or child in the war, and then you will see why the answer has to be yes."

"I think the answer has to be no," I said. "Ask yourself this question, Avram. Should I really stop going to The Bargain Buggy with Katya because her father lived in a country where a madman took over?"

Avram slowly nodded his head. "You should certainly consider it." Then he switched to a more neutral tone and pointed indoors. "We'd better go inside." He began to walk in the direction of the crafts room. "Just think about it, Rachel. You should consider my advice very seriously."

Eight

The shoulds. Everyone had a suggestion for me about how I *should* be, what I *should* do, the way I *should* think. *They should leave me alone,* I decided. I was waiting for Katya to come out of her house so we could bike to The Bargain Buggy together. Her mother (her *German* mother) had just come to the door to say Katya would be out in a minute.

"But do me a favor," she said. "You girls — don't ride on Santa Anita, it's too dangerous." She went in. Then she came to the door a second time to offer me a piece of apple cake. I took a slice and thanked her. Avram's face came to mind as I bit into the cake: Could it be she wanted to poison me? Was Mrs. Ohlendorf my enemy?

The shoulds. Should I really not be here, taking cake from a woman who might have waved at Hitler? Where should I be? *What* should I be? If I left it up to other people, they'd know exactly how to hammer me into shape. Everyone seemed to know without doubt what I should be. Mom would say I should be a fashion plate and be more ladylike. Daddy would say I should commit to some profession (where I would make a lot of money and be world-famous) before another instant passed by, not to mention that I should marry a Jewish man. Franny would say I should *never* marry, and Erica would say I should marry tomorrow, considering how dreamily happy she was these days, now that her wedding to Harlan was only a matter of weeks away.

Katya came clattering out the front door, yelling good-bye to people inside. She stuck her head back in the doorway. "You want to come with us, Karl?" she called.

"I can't, I have to hang upside down," I heard someone say.

"Come look at my crazy brother," Katya called to me. I walked up a couple of steps and peered in the front door. Karl was hanging upside down on some contraption in the doorway between the living room and the dining room. His face was beet-red, and his blond hair, the same color as Katya's, hung straight down like a short, shimmering curtain. He saw me staring at him. I was trying to make sense of his blue eyes staring at me from the bottom of his head and his mouth talking at me from the top.

"It brings the blood to my brain and makes me smarter," he said. "Want to try it, Rachel?"

"No thanks, I'm already a genius," I said. "There's nothing in it for me."

"He's nuts," Katya said affectionately.

"It's from the yeast I work with at bakers' college," he said, defending himself. "This yeast causes a deadly mutation that turns the brain into a mass of wet Twinkies. You want a turn? It's fun."

I noticed he didn't say, "You *should* try it." I was grateful.

"See you later," Katya said. "I'll try to bring you a present from The Bargain Buggy."

Katya and I got in rhythm pedaling down Santa Anita (in spite of what Katya's mother had said) till we were going fast and right in synch. Our hair blew in the wind, and we rode side by side for a while till we had to separate and go single file, because the traffic was really heavy. Santa Anita was the road to the racetrack, and on Saturday mornings it got really wild out there.

"Did your mom make you wear your dog tags?" I yelled to Katya. We had our worrisome mothers in common. When Katya was in first grade, her mother ordered, from some ID company, a silver dog tag with her name, address, and phone number on it, plus her religion and her blood type. In elementary and junior high school, she had to wear it every day. Now that she was in high school, she only had to wear it when she went on class trips, or to the ice-skating rink, or to the beach, and whenever she rode her bike.

"I'm wearing the subs," she called back to me over her shoulder. She meant the substitute dog tags she once found in The Bargain Buggy in a pile of old junk. The tags had the name of a soldier from World War II on them: Lieutenant Henry Sherman. This little deceit was the way Katya got around feeling imprisoned; she wore her fake dog tags. My way was to throw out my bras and wear black clothes. I wasn't altogether sure that this would be a permanent thing with me, but I felt it was absolutely necessary now.

Katya squealed in delight when she saw that The Bargain Buggy had its belly-dancer mannequin outside the door. It meant it was Stuff-Your-Bag day; we were really in luck. We locked our bikes around a street sign pole, stopped to admire a big black motorcycle parked at the curb, and went inside.

"That smell," Katya said. She inhaled, as if it were the rarest perfume. I liked it, too — a combination of dust and wool and old leather and maybe clothing and furniture that wasn't too clean. We both agreed that the smell here was much nicer than the smell at Fashion Mall, which was made up of ammonia-sharp window cleaner and plastic display cases and new shoes and the ink on newly printed DRASTIC SALE signs.

"I'm dying to find a red velvet cape. I better hurry before someone else finds one ahead of me," Katya said. We had both bought empty paper bags from a woman called Faith, who worked at the desk. She always wore a flaming red curly wig that she had once taken out of the wig bin. She once confided to us that she liked it better than her regular hair.

Katya rushed off to find some treasures. I was in no hurry to race to the black-shirt rack — no one ever raided that department. Everything in The Bargain Buggy was arranged by colors, not by sizes. I meandered around, bypassing the Designer Rack (too expensive — things there were $5 and up!). I examined the bins of knickknacks, the games, the old combs and wallets and sunglasses and Ace bandages.

On the New Arrivals table was a pink cashmere sweater with just a few tiny moth holes; it had a real mink collar. Not just a fur collar, but a *mink* collar, the whole animal — the mink itself — was attached with its head, its eyes, and its sharp little teeth. Its silky tail curled below, coming to rest against some tiny buttons. I would never buy a dead animal to wear around my neck; it was against my principles. But I touched the fur, thinking of an age in which this article of clothing was considered glamorous and fancy. I imagined a woman in an ankle-length slinky dress wearing it at a party, holding her cigarette in a long cigarette holder. She could never pull that off now. She'd be run out the door by nonsmokers and animal-rights activists!

I checked the stuffed animal bins, the old purses bins, the bathing suits and tennis dresses bins, the toaster and frying pan shelves, the hat racks, the old cameras drawer, the wallpaper rolls, the broken clock-and-radio shelves.

Here and there I chose something and dropped it into my bag — a glass perfume atomizer with a netlike wrapping around it. I loved perfume, though Franny said it was just a lure for men, and who would want to lure men?

I put in a plaster statue of a gold angel with wings. I added a pair of black patent-leather stiletto high heels, and a Snoopy-dog jigsaw puzzle. I loved grown-up stuff and cute kid stuff. I had a lot of contradictions in my nature, but I figured that was okay: My nature was not yet set for life.

"Hey, look!" Katya called from the back of the shop. She was opening a paper parasol and twirling it over her head. Behind her, through the glare of sunlight coming in the back door, I could see the big items they kept in the outside yard: washing machines, shower doors, swing sets, broken lamps, animal cages.

I made my way to the Book Nook, which was my favorite part of The Bargain Buggy. Its cozy corner reminded me of the reading area in my third-grade classroom: a couple of beanbag chairs (with a few holes from which white Styrofoam beads spilled), an old couch, and an overstuffed feather-and-down chair that I loved to sink into. My mother hated it every time I came home with another dozen paperbacks or so. But for ten cents each, why wouldn't I want to improve my library? She thought books with ripped-off covers and torn edges made my room look like a slum.

Some guy was sitting in my favorite chair; he had a wild unruly head of curls and a long sensitive face. He looked about nineteen. His long legs were stretched way out in front of him, and he was reading a tattered copy of *Zen and the Art of Motorcycle Maintenance*. My heart sank when I saw a black wool shirt hanging over the arm of his chair, with the Bargain Buggy price tag still on it. I sighed involuntarily. What a disappointment! It was a gorgeous black Pendleton wool shirt with a silk lining. (I had seen it last week, but it had been on the Designer Rack, which was out of my price range.) Now it was marked down and had the regular green price tag. That meant it was like everything else in the store: You could stuff it on Stuff-Your-Bag day.

Darn! It was just what I wanted. I could have worn it to school every day in the winter. If I got to go to The Mountainside School it would be perfect for months of living on a bus! The application had arrived very fast. I had it on my bedside table. I had to write an essay on "Why I think I would benefit from spending senior year in The Mountainside School, and how my goals and aspirations will benefit the school."

Without even realizing I was going to do this, I stepped over to the chair and actually stroked the sleeve of the shirt.

"Hmm, hello?" The guy looked up and smiled. He had blue eyes and the sweetest face. I was reminded of Karl's blue eyes, upside down, and his face, which wasn't exactly sweet but more elflike, mischievous. I like to think about guys' faces and their bodies, too. Something else Franny didn't approve of. She didn't think bodies should be considered separate from the whole person. The fact is, when you first met a guy, you didn't *know* his inner soul. All you saw was his body — and that's all he saw when he first met you.

This guy was looking at me, but not at my body. I mean, you can tell the difference.

"I'm wondering if this is your shirt," I said.

"I'm considering it," he said. "It's not bad, is it?"

"It has moth holes in it," I informed him. I didn't even have to look; every wool shirt at The Bargain Buggy has moth holes in it. Unless, of course, the owner died, but in that case, in the case of a perfect shirt, some relative would probably keep it.

"Is that serious?" the guy asked me.

"Moth holes usually get bigger."

"No kidding. I don't know much about moths."

"If there are still larvae in the wool," I added, "it'll probably turn into one major black hole."

"I could wash it to get them out," he said dubiously. "The hot water would probably do it."

"You don't want to do *that!* Hot water will ruin wool."

"You seem to know a lot about these things."

"I'm an expert on black wool," I told him. "I wear only natural fibers, and only the color black."

"Then this shirt is right up your alley, isn't it?"

"It's magnificent," I said. I bent down and lifted the sleeve up to my cheek.

"Look, if you like it that much, you can have

it," he said. "I'm not that keen on it since it's full of moth eggs, anyway."

"Thank you!" I cried. "You don't know how I appreciate this! It isn't so easy to find everything you need in black."

He settled back to read his book. It was then that I noticed all the other books strewn around his feet: *The Way of Zen, The Three Pillars of Zen, What Is Zen, The Method of Zen.*

He looked up at me.

"I guess you're into Zen," I said. I couldn't believe how stupid that sounded.

"I'm learning. I was lucky to find all these books here today. Understanding Zen is a very slow process."

"I'm pretty slow in certain areas, too," I said, "especially physics and chemistry."

"I'm not bad at that stuff," he said, "or at least I wasn't when I was studying. I used to want to be an astronomer."

"But you don't anymore?"

He shook his head. "I dropped out of school."

"What do you want now?"

"I try not to want anything. I do odd jobs to stay afloat, and I wander the world."

"Is that why you gave me the shirt? Because you didn't want to want it?"

"No, that was easy," he said. "It's the other stuff that it's hard not to want. Success, power, you know. . . ."

"*I* want all that stuff," I said. "Who doesn't? I mean, that's what your parents tell you from the start. 'Be the best, get ahead.' "

"Yeah," he said. "The old poison."

"So what can you do instead?"

"Try to achieve *satori* — or enlightenment. Wisdom."

"It sounds interesting," I said, although I wasn't really sure.

"Here, take this book, you might enjoy it." He handed me the one titled *The Method of Zen*. On the cover, a single weeping-willow branch was silhouetted against a pale red sun. Or moon. It was hard to tell which. I opened the book at random and read a sentence someone had underlined in pencil: *The finger pointing at the moon is not the moon itself.*

I read the sentence out loud. "What does this mean?" I asked him.

He smiled at me. "Who knows?" he said. "That's what I'm trying to learn. The meaning of meaning."

Just then Katya came swirling by in a red velvet cape and black boots. She was swinging a belt and looked like a lion tamer. "Look what I found!" she said. Then she saw my friend and added, "Look what *you* found!"

I actually blushed. Then I introduced them, sort of, since I didn't even know his name.

"Jason," he said, holding out his hand. He shook Katya's hand, and I felt a twinge of something, maybe jealousy, since he hadn't shaken mine.

"Rachel," I said, holding out my hand.

"Very good," Jason said, reaching for my hand and squeezing it warmly.

"You ready to go?" Katya said.

"Oh — just give me a minute to fill up my bag."

I dashed off. Now that the wonderful shirt was in it, I hardly needed anything else. But I grabbed a few more black items — a black leather belt, a black silk scarf, black wool mittens.

Jason held up the book as I came toward them. "Don't forget this; I think you'd appreciate it." He handed it to me. "I come here pretty often," he said. "The books are great. Maybe I'll see you here some other time?"

"I come every Saturday," I said.

"She comes without fail," Katya said. I could have kicked her.

"Good, so I'll see you sometime. Maybe if you get interested in Zen, you'll want to come to the Zen Center up on Mt. Baldy with me. See how they do things."

"Could be," I said.

"That isn't your bike outside, is it?" Katya asked. "That big Yamaha motorcycle?"

"That's my trusty steed," Jason said.

"Wow," Katya said.

"No kidding," I said. I was beginning to think this encounter was getting a little out of hand.

"Is that what you'd take Rachel up the mountain on?" Katya asked.

I did kick her. "Come on," I said. To Jason, I added, "Nice to have met you."

"See you next Saturday," he said to me.

"She'll be here," Katya said.

Nine

I was in the darkroom Saturday night when Erica knocked.

"I know you can't open the door," she said. "But Katya just called and said to give you a message."

"What's the message?"

"She said to tell you: 'He's adorable.' "

"Thanks," I said.

"Who's adorable, Rachel?"

"Oh, no one, really."

"Ra-a-a-chel, you're keeping a secret from me."

"Honestly, Erica. It was just some guy we met

in the thrift shop." I heard the doorknob turn. "No, Erica! Don't open the door — I have prints in the tray!"

"Then tell me more."

"What's so important about some guy?"

"Because love is important. I think it's time you fell in love. You're sixteen already."

"Don't start on that love stuff, Erica. You have no sense of reality these days. All you have on your mind is wedding bells."

"Without a man to love, you are not complete," Erica called to me. Even though she said it through the closed door, even though she had to sort of yell it, it came out dreamy and kind of dazed.

"I'm glad you're so happy," I said. "But I have to do these photos now. I'll talk to you a little later."

I heard Erica go down the hall. From her room, I heard music. She was playing a tape by Harlan's favorite group, The Shrunken Heads, whose music was really very weird, in my opinion. All their songs had only one word. Involuntarily I had so far heard their hit songs many times: "Passion," "Trouble," "Rescue," and "Disaster." A whole song, with the word "passion" as its only lyric could get pretty monotonous — even though the group sang it to drums, harmonicas, harps, and trombones. Even though they had little fluttering angel voices doing the harmony. Even though the song called "Disaster" ended with what sounded like some member of the group choking to death. This stuff was the favorite music of Erica's husband-to-be, who otherwise was a very sweet, mild-mannered guy who was a computer programmer.

Actually, they were a terribly traditional couple. Erica was planning to register her silver and crystal and china patterns at Bullock's, and she and Harlan had already bought matching wedding bands. Her girlfriends were giving her a wedding shower at The Pink Onion restaurant. The only thing out-of-the-ordinary was the wedding on the mountain they were planning, but I guess it sounded romantic to them — Scottish bagpipes and guys in kilts and all that stuff. Well, I supposed Erica might as well have one big romantic extravaganza before she settled down to making rice casseroles and microwave brownies.

For myself — I had a different life in mind. It was just coming into focus, like the photos of my cats, Itzhak and Basil, as they came to life in the developing fluid. I peered into the tray. Slowly the images were coming forth. Like ghosts, they were taking bodily shape.

I loved it here in my darkroom — it was my refuge, my safe harbor. I loved the dull orange glow of the safelight; it made the darkness warm and delicious. My enlarger looked like a benign prehistoric monster or, depending how I looked at it, it sometimes appeared to be a clown with a little tin head and a long accordian face.

The best thing about my darkroom was that no one dared to walk in — even my mother. That's because she couldn't help but read the *humongous* sign I'd taped to the door:

My parents understood the word "ruined," especially if whatever could be ruined had cost a lot of money. Film would go to waste, and that wasn't good. After all, hadn't they spent a fortune on buying me film? The enlarger? A timer? Tongs? Chemicals? Developing fluid?

It was sad to think of them passing the darkroom door and whispering to each other, "Oh, good, she's in there. Maybe she's on the right track *now*. Maybe she's going to get serious *now* and become a world-famous photographer!"

On the days I didn't use the darkroom, I imagined them saying to each other, "What a pity, so much money down the drain. We got her all that equipment, and she isn't showing any interest in it."

Why did they think everything I tried was a waste if I didn't pledge my life to it? They simply didn't understand the nature of my investigation. A young person needed to go around trying on lives. I might still become a great ornithologist — how could I be sure yet?

It wasn't a waste of time if I gave something up and moved on to another interest. After all, I had had to give up my dollhouse and my marbles in the natural order of things, and my parents didn't see *that* as some great betrayal. Then why were they always making fusses over all the "equipment" with which they provided me — if it didn't yield immediate results?

I could see my photograph now, coming clear. It was Itzhak and Basil staring at the devil chaser, which I had leaned against a tree in the backyard. The devil chaser had belonged to my grandfather, who had found the object — he thought it was a piece of primitive art — among some cartons of stuff he had bought for his antique store. He had died young of leukemia before I was born (though my mother tells me I look like him: she says I have his eyebrows and his nose and the same slant of his cheekbones).

The devil's head was carved out of wood; the devil's face was painted red, with a sharp black beard. The head was set on a long pole, and up at the top was a set of cymbals, balanced just above the devil's pointed ears. Maybe natives of some tribe in a faraway jungle had used it hundreds of years ago to scare away evil spirits. (I don't guess my grandfather was able to scare away his disease with it, though.)

The devil chaser was the strangest thing I owned, and my parents were always after me to hide it away in the garage. Even though my grandfather had owned it, they thought it was "gruesome and unwholesome." The thing is, I loved looking at it. Sometimes I half believed in spirits and souls and auras and reincarnation.

I would never discuss this with my parents — they would think I was crazy. My mother would feel my forehead, and my father would try to distract me with garbage-can carrying. But I knew things existed in me and in the world that had nothing to do with the practical events of everyday life. There were things I felt — like fear and wonder and joy and hope — that had nothing sensible or practical about them.

The devil's face was coming clear in the tray. I loved this moment when I finally got down to developing my film after putting it off for days and days. Finally, once I got into it, I had this tremendous sense of purpose. I felt I had started something irrevocable; the second I was into the work, nothing could stop me. For a change, I didn't worry about my face or my hair or my troubles or my future life. I just did what I had to do.

I wished I had the discipline to get into hard work more often because, when I did finally focus my attention, I found I had much more energy and lots of new ideas. I discovered some sort of strange reserve of power — I could stay up late, lose track of time, but I didn't get tired. I felt as if the more I did, the more I *could* do!

Usually it was easier not to do it, just to sit around dreaming, or eating cheese and crackers, or listening to music. But when I finally got the wheels turning, I was energized, elated. Once "my little boyfriend" Rick had called when I was in a state of power and enthusiasm like that and said to me on the phone, "You sound like you just smoked three joints."

That's how much he knew. That's just about how much everyone knows. Why is everyone so incredibly thick? That's what I'd like to know!

Ten

I had two men-of-ideas in my life, and I thought I should bone up on their interests. For Avram, I had pulled the *Encyclopedia of Judaism* out of the bookcase and dumped the huge volume beside my bed. For Jason, to be prepared for when I would next see him (on Saturday, I hoped, at The Bargain Buggy), I was trying to read *The Method of Zen*. It wasn't easy to get a firm grasp on two great world religions in a half hour of reading.

It didn't help when Franny knocked and charged into my room when I said, "Come in." She was waving a little pink child's book in the air.

"Will you look at this?" she asked. "Erica was

packing up stuff to take away after her wedding, and she wants to keep this book for her children-to-be."

"So? What's wrong with that? Did it used to be yours, or what?"

"It used to be all of ours!" Franny said. She plopped down on my bed. "I can't believe we were fed this junk."

I took the book from her hand; oh, yes, I remembered it very well. It was called *I Can Be Anything* and featured the joys of a little girl trying to decide among three careers: Should she be a ballerina, a nurse, or an airline stewardess? For a time I had decided I'd be a ballerina, till I realized I couldn't do a backbend, no less a split. Then I picked nurse, but I really didn't enjoy the idea of pulling bandages off wounds. A stewardess wasn't too bad, because you got to wear a cute little hat.

"Books like this should be outlawed!" Franny said. "They distort the minds of young girls."

"But young girls grow up, and then they read other stuff," I said.

"Like what?"

I knew I was in for trouble when Franny started looking at my present reading material.

"Why on earth are you reading this stuff?" she demanded.

I considered telling her I wanted to expand my spiritual horizons, but you can't lie to Franny. "I know two guys who are interested in religion," I admitted. "They're not both interested in both religions; I mean — one is a rabbinical student, and one is into Zen."

"Which guy are *you* into?" Franny said, because she's very astute.

"I'm not sure. I think the Zen guy is very gentle and very nice. The other one is head counselor at the day camp — I told you about him. He's the one who's going to be a rabbi."

"Which one is cuter?" Franny said. She likes to zero in on essential issues.

"Both cute, both different," I said. It was easier to talk to Franny than to Erica, because she didn't have any kind of dreamy haze around her head.

"But tell me, Rachel — " she said, flopping down on my bed, grabbing one of my pillows, and stuffing it under her arm. Her long hair fanned out over the pillow, catching the light from my reading lamp. " — are you reading this stuff because you're interested in it, or because some *guy* you're interested in is interested in it?"

"What's the difference?"

"Big difference, little sister," she said. "We women don't do that anymore." She mimicked some imaginary airhead: " 'Oh, Jimmy, how wonderful that you love baseball! Well, guess what? Would you believe it? I'm a big baseball fan, too!' or 'Oh, Bill, I'd be just *thrilled* to learn about car engines! I've always adored carburetors!' Rachel, we just don't play games like that if we have any sense."

"Zen is not a ball game." I defended myself. "It's a system of thought. I'm trying to find out what I think about things! Don't you think I ought to investigate every possibility?"

I stuck my book out to Franny. "Look at this,"

I said. I read aloud: " 'The disciple of Buddha may not love in the ordinary sense of the word and in the end cannot do so. . . . He lets everybody have a share in his rich capacity for loving, without counting on any love in return.' Do you think that means that a man who's into Zen can't fall in love with a woman?"

"That's sure what it sounds like," she said. "It's a little ominous to me."

"What about orthodox rabbis? Can they fall in love?"

"From the looks of all their little children," Franny said, "it seems they must do a good approximation of it."

"You don't sound very respectful, Franny."

"It's hard to have respect for a religion in which women are viewed as less than equals. The wives of orthodox rabbis have one job and that's to have lots of babies and to stay home and mind the house. Period!"

"But that's only among the orthodox, and they actually think women have a very *important* job in the home, to raise the children properly and teach them the values of Jewish family life." I held up the encyclopedia, to give weight to my claim. I realized I was coming to Avram's defense, although I really didn't sympathize with his position very much. "If you think about Mom and Dad's friends who are orthodox, none of the women are 'inferior.' "

"But it's not them I'm worried about," Franny said. "It's you. If you let yourself be swept off your feet by an orthodox rabbinical student, there's no telling where you may end up. You may end up walking ten feet behind him, adoring his coattails."

"Not me," I assured Franny. "Not me. Do I look like the type?"

I jumped off my bed and straddled my desk chair to show Franny how liberated I was. She laughed. Then she came over and hugged me.

"Just remember you're a whole person," she said to me. "Don't let anyone stick you in any cubbyholes and label you."

She scooted off my bed and started looking at the stuff on my dresser. A stuffed owl, several perfume atomizers, lots of dried-out marking pens, an Etch-A-Sketch, two boxes of hardened gummy bears, a . . .

"What's this?" Franny demanded. She held up one of my purchases from The Bargain Buggy, a black lace garter belt.

"Put that down, Franny!"

"Come on! Did you buy this? Would you ever wear it?"

"Maybe. I don't know. Someday, maybe. I'm not going to wear black sweatpants forever."

"You should!" Franny said. "If I had to wear a thing like that, I'd strangle myself with it first!"

Eleven

"Why do you always wear black, Rachel?"

Avram and I were sitting in the rabbi's study, eating falafel in pita bread — a project we had made with the kids during "Creative Cooking Hour." Now the kids were having their creations for lunch, and some CITs were looking after them.

"I get along well with black," I said. "It suits my state of mind these days." I looked at his face to see if he might understand what I meant.

"Rabbi Gelber asked me the other day if you were in mourning or something."

"Well, tell him not to worry, it's nothing like that.

I just feel it expresses something in my nature."

I pointed to Avram's pants. "*You* always wear black pants."

"I dress in a tradition," he said. "I *live* in a tradition."

"Your tradition doesn't give you much leeway, does it?" I asked him.

"On the contrary," he said, "living within a structure allows you to develop other areas of your life to the fullest. You don't have to worry about the basics then — they're taken care of."

He looked very wise when he said that; my heart gave a little skip. He might not understand my motives for dressing in black, but he was very certain about the things that he did understand. I thought, in a way, he was very lucky. Whoever he married — (why was I thinking about marriage? It must have had something to do with this wedding of Erica's looming over all of us!) — whoever he married would have everything decided for her: how to dress, how to live, how to think, how to conduct herself, how to raise her children. What a load off my mind it would be if I never had to worry about all that stuff!

"I'm reading the *Encyclopedia of Judaism* these days," I said to Avram. He looked impressed, which was what I was after.

"Are you really serious about studying Jewish law and history?" he asked. "Would you like me to help you?"

"Oh, I would, I would," I said. "I'd like to learn more about the religious life. Except . . ."

"Orthodox family life is very joyous, Rachel,"

66

he interrupted. "You have to see it to understand." He saw that my cup was empty and took the pitcher of red punch off the desk and poured me a cupful. The punch bubbled in, a layer of foam spread over the top of my cup. I felt touched, as if he had suddenly done some chivalrous thing for me.

"I'll tell you what, Rachel," he said. "Next weekend my cousin Yeheuda is getting married in Los Angeles. Would you like to come to an orthodox wedding? I think you'd be very impressed. It might change your whole way of viewing life. You might begin to see it my way."

"Next weekend? What day?" I said. I was planning to go to The Bargain Buggy on Saturday in the hopes of finding Jason there. And his motorcycle. No wedding was going to interfere with that!

"Sunday," Avram said. "It would have to be Sunday," he said, with a little critical blink, "because we wouldn't have a wedding on the Sabbath. We couldn't even get there because we're not allowed to drive on the Sabbath."

"Sorry," I said. I felt ignorant, and then I felt annoyed. Avram knew I wasn't an expert on Jewish orthodoxy, so why should he expect me to be aware of the finer points? On the other hand, I had a feeling that this was a *very* basic point — not so fine — and I should have known it. Why was I so anxious that Avram think well of me?

"So will you come with me to Yeheuda's wedding? Maybe someday you will want to have a wedding just like hers."

With you? I thought. "That sounds good. I'd love to go. And then maybe you can come to my sister

Erica's wedding. She's getting married at the end of August."

Avram seemed to recoil a little.

"Is Rabbi Gelber going to marry her?"

"No — she and her boyfriend are doing it themselves. I mean, there's no rabbi or anything, just the birds and the bees. I mean the trees. He's not Jewish," I added, feeling oddly flustered.

Avram made a slightly sour face, as if he'd found something that tasted bad in his pita bread.

"A pity about your sister," he said.

"It's not such a pity! I mean, she's very happy right now, even if her boyfriend does adore The Shrunken Heads."

"You know why it's a pity?" Avram said, ignoring my last comment. "Because it can't work."

"It's working now. All over America. All over the world."

"Yes — well, I'm talking about in the long run. The wisdom of the ages has proved it; it's best to marry your own kind."

I was trying to think of an answer to that (*Oh, Franny, where are you?* I begged her), but just then our star troublemaking camper, Danny, crashed into the room and yelled that Harriet had pulled down the trampoline and accidentally spilled her punch all over it.

"By the way," Avram called to me as he hurried away to attend to the emergency, "if we don't get a chance to talk about this again, I'll pick you up at your house on Sunday, at eleven A.M. Of course you know that for an orthodox wedding you have to be modestly dressed — long sleeves, high neck

. . . I hope you have something suitable."

Then he was gone.

"How about a long, black, hooded flannel nightshirt?" I mumbled after him. "Maybe tied with a black karate belt?"

Twelve

Early Saturday morning, I was combing my hair and admiring myself in the black Pendelton wool shirt I had put on to wear to The Bargain Buggy when my mother barged into my room.

"Where do you think you're going today, young lady?" she asked, and gave me one of her I-can't-believe-I-have-to-put-up-with-it looks. "Don't tell me you're really going to wear that ridiculously heavy shirt? Do you know how hot and smoggy it is today?"

"I like to feel insulated," I explained. "And in about an hour I'm going to meet Katya and see what treasures we can dig up at The Bargain Buggy."

"The cats need work," my mother said.

"The cats need work?"

"They need new flea collars. And they need rabies shots, which they haven't had in nearly two years. I wanted you and Franny to take them to the vet for shots today. Daddy says 'possums have been drinking from their water bowls at night. Wild animals can spread rabies, you know. There's an excellent chance the cats will get rabies and then give the disease to all of us!"

"They won't get rabies right this minute, Mom. I mean — I'll do it soon — we can take the cats to the vet during the week if Franny will drive. We can do it after camp one day. But I can't do it today."

"Maybe you can drive the cats yourself," my mother said slyly.

"What do you mean? I don't have my license yet. Daddy keeps refusing to take me for my test."

"He'll take you today," my mother said, dropping this bombshell at my feet. "Right now, in fact. I've convinced him it's time."

"How come?"

"Because with Franny sick, I really need you to do certain errands this summer, and how can you, if you can't drive the car?"

"That's what I've been saying all along. But he hates to get in the car with me. I did perfectly well in driver's training at school, but he thinks I'm death on wheels."

"He said he'll take you right now," my mother said. "I wouldn't let the moment pass."

"Okay," I agreed. "Let me call Katya and tell her I'll go out with her a little later." (I figured that if Jason were at The Bargain Buggy, he'd be there all morning, reading books.) "Tell Daddy to put on his crash helmet."

"You're going to hit that pole," my father said. "Hit the brake! Hit the brake!"

"What pole?" I asked, slowing down the old Plymouth. "The only thing I see is a tree across the street."

"That's what I mean," my father said, taking his handkerchief from his pocket and wiping his brow. "You were much too close."

I bit my lip. I had learned never to debate with my father during these encounters. It was far better simply to brake every three seconds and allow him to think he was saving our lives. Riding with him was very jerky; jerking along this way to the DMV was going to take at least a half hour, though normally it would be about a ten-minute ride.

"Slow down," he yelled, grabbing the armrest.

"I'm only going eight miles an hour. Nothing serious can happen."

"I know," he said. "I have complete confidence in you, Rachel. You know that." He glanced forward and cried, "Hit the brake!"

I pulled over to the curb. "Daddy," I said, "wouldn't you hate it if I were driving with you, and every second I yelled out, 'Hit the brake! Hit the brake!'?"

"Yes," he said, "but — "

"So give me a chance to get us there alive. If you have confidence in me, be quiet."

"All right," he agreed. "I'm a reasonable man."

"Okay, here I go." I began to pull out into traffic, first checking the rearview mirror, then the side-view mirror, then signaling, then creeping out so slowly that a car started honking. We drove a full fifty seconds in silence, my father trying to stifle his gasps.

"Hang on, Daddy," I warned him. "I'm going to make a very slow right turn."

"Don't go up on the curb," he breathed, as if he were saying a prayer.

"I won't," I said, and then I felt my rear wheels scrape the curb. Just when I didn't want to get nervous, I was feeling myself lose faith that I could pass the test. I thought my father would make me turn around and go home. But he seemed to have passed out. In any case, his head was lolling back against the seat and his eyes were closed. I took advantage of the occurrence to accelerate to a normal speed of about fifteen miles per hour, and thereby cover the rest of the distance to the DMV before nightfall.

"We're here, Daddy," I said.

"Thank God." He opened the door and tumbled out.

"I know just what to do," I assured my father. "You can just sit down on a bench and rest. All my friends have done this. I just go in and give them my driver's-training slip, signed by my teacher, and show them my permit, and then I get to drive with an examiner."

"Okay, sure." He waved me away and staggered to a wooden bench. Inside it was a madhouse. It was as if everyone in America wanted to start driving today. I saw old people with canes, and kids with portable stereos, and pregnant women, and tough-looking men with tattoos on their arms. I got on a long line. It moved slowly along. Other people on line were listening to their Walkmans, some were reading magazines, others were cramming from the driving manual. One man even had a tiny portable TV held up to his face. I thought about my birds, my darkroom, about Avram, about Jason. Luckily, I had the riches of my mind to entertain me!

The examiner for my driver's test turned out to be a perfectly ordinary sourpuss who barely nodded hello, and who — the instant he got in the car — started making nasty pencil marks on this clipboard.

I did everything by the book. I fastened my seat belt, adjusted my seat, my rearview mirror, my sideview mirror. I looked at the examiner, sitting there with his wire-rim glasses and his crew-cut hair, frowning.

"Shall I go?" I asked.

He grunted.

I could see my father, with his eyes still closed, on the bench. I wondered if he might be having a heart attack. I had intended to smile at him and wave, but his attention could not be attracted. *Con-*

centrate, Rachel, he had said. I decided to put everything out of my mind but the steering wheel, the brake, and the turn signal.

We pulled out into the street, and the examiner was making frantic notes on his clipboard. We drove directly to a railroad crossing where I stopped and looked both ways. Out of the corner of my eye, I saw him make an "x" in some column. I wanted to say, *Look, I'm in a very nervous state, don't be too hard to me*. But of course I knew that wouldn't hold water. *He* might be right in the middle of a divorce or something. We all had problems. We couldn't ask for special favors. Franny had told me that it would be all over if I hit another car, hit a pedestrian, hit a pole, or drove up onto the sidewalk. I wondered what would happen if I ran over a pigeon. There were several streets in our city that were full of birds, for some reason. They were fat and waddly, and could barely fly up over the hoods of cars. I prayed we wouldn't end up on one of those streets. I hated the thought of squashed birds.

"Left turn," he grunted.

I turned. He scribbled.

"Back up over there," he grunted.

I backed up. My shirt was soaked.

"Emergency vehicle coming," he mumbled.

Sirens! I dreaded sirens. I never knew which way they were coming from. Franny said the worst thing was to be in an intersection and hear sirens, and not to know whether to stop or go.

An ice cream truck passed. It had a big red plastic

bullhorn on its roof and was blasting out an ear-splitting siren sound.

"They think they're Cheech and Chong," he grumbled. He jotted down their license. "They'll be sorry," he said with satisfaction. After that he seemed vaguely cheerful, and even smiled at me once when I looked in his direction.

"Wise guys," he said.

I nodded agreement.

"We need to get people like that off the road."

"Oh, yes," I said.

"Teenagers," he said.

I wondered what he thought I was.

"Left turn," he advised. "Back to the ranch."

When I pulled into the parking lot of the DMV, he directed me to a parking space.

"Well, young lady," he said. "You just go right inside now and hand in those papers to window twenty-four, and you're all set."

I was all set!

"Good luck, young lady. I'm sure you'll be a credit to the young drivers of America."

"And thank you," I said and added generously, "I think *you're* a credit to the driver's-license testers of America."

Triumphantly, I drove my father home. As soon as he got in the house, he took a tranquilizer and went to bed. Luckily, my mother had forgotten all about the "work on the cats."

"Katya called," she said. "She says to give her a call when you're ready to go."

"Can I use the car to drive to The Bargain Buggy?" I asked.

76

"Not so fast! Just because you have your license now doesn't mean you can have the car any old time."

"Perish the thought," I said. "I'll take my bike."

"But if you *do* take the car, maybe you can do some food shopping for me," she added. "And run down to the dry cleaners. . . ."

" 'Bye, Mom," I said. "I'm off. . . . I'll take the car another time."

"You really don't need any more black clothing," my mother warned me. "Why not look around for something in fuchsia, or tangerine, something bright?"

"I'll give it serious thought," I said. "I really will."

He was there! I knew the instant I saw the big, black motorcycle that he was inside. The bike seemed enormous, like a great animal at rest. I felt thrilled, just to look at it.

Katya punched my shoulder. "You'll probably get to ride on that thing, you lucky dog," she said.

"I doubt it," I told her, chaining my bike. "Just don't say anything to embarrass me, okay?"

She grinned. "What could I possibly say?"

"You," I told her, "are capable of anything, in your innocent way."

"Oh, by the way, my brother, Karl, sends regards," she said. "He told me to bring you home for dinner. He's baking some special bread this afternoon — he wants to offer you a taste of his talents."

"Is he hanging upside down today?" I asked.

"That's not all he does," Katya said. "He's not crazy, you know. He's a very neat guy."

"Also cute," I added.

"Not as cute as what's-his-name!" She pointed into The Bargain Buggy, and I punched her.

Now my heart was really beginning to pound. Before this, I had felt cool — if Jason were there, fine. If not, fine. But now I knew he was really inside, that he might have come just to see me, and I didn't feel cool at all.

He was sitting in that same chair, this time wearing a cowboy hat (with a Bargain Buggy price tag hanging from the brim) and reading. As if he had been waiting for me, he looked up just as I looked over at him, and he smiled. It was the kind of smile you probably get only a few times in this life, I thought — a great smile, a totally welcoming, accepting, happiness-giving smile. He was completely, wholly, glad to see me.

I headed right for him. I left Katya standing there and just went over to him, stumbling over some books on the floor by his feet.

"Howdy," he said, tipping his cowboy hat, and I laughed. My laugh was too loud, but there it was.

He held out his hand, and I took it — but it wasn't a handshake we exchanged, it was more like a hug between fingers.

"Guess what I saw on the black rack? A great black Burberry winter coat," he said. "From London, England. Want to see it?"

"It's too hot in California for that," I said. "It's

going to be eighty-eight degrees today." For an instant, I sounded just like my mother. This always horrified me, the way her voice and her words simply popped out of my mouth.

"But maybe someday you'll travel to the Himalayas," Jason said, his eyebrows rising. "That's where I'd like to go someday. Those snowcapped mountains. It's best to be prepared, don't you think?"

"It's just that I already have too much stuff in my closet," I said.

"We all have too much stuff," he agreed. "I'm trying to learn to travel light. I'm trying to learn how to get along without so many possessions. Buddha said that possessions are what destroy us."

"I guess that includes your motorcycle," I said. "That's a mighty major possession."

"You got me there," he said, pointing his index finger at me. "I guess I'm still pretty far from achieving nirvana," he told me. "I have a long way to go to travel as a free spirit."

"What's nirvana?"

"That's the highest achievement of Zen," he said. "Nirvana is all desires met; there's no need for desires."

Just then Katya called my name from the back of the store. "Rachel — they've got the cutest birdhouse out back. It's made of wicker, and it has about ten little floors, like a bird skyscraper."

"I think I'm out of my bird stage." I called back, "but I'll come look anyway."

Jason reached toward me and touched my arm.

"Can you spare a couple of hours?"

"Why?"

"I thought maybe you'd like to visit the monastery on the mountain. They welcome beginners every weekend. We can sit *zazen* with them, and do walking meditation, and have vegetarian lunch with the monks."

"What's *zazen*?" I waved to Katya to indicate that I'd be there in a minute.

"Well, it's a formal sitting practice they do. They give us pillows and show us how to breathe and sit. It's a way of quieting the mind. And they're very happy to have interested guests come and visit."

"I'm not sure I want to quiet my mind," I said. "It's interesting in there when it's busy and noisy."

"Don't knock it till you try it."

"All right," I agreed, "I'll try it."

"Great. Can we leave in about ten minutes?"

"I'll have to tell Katya. Can I ride my bike there?"

"It's up a *mountain*," Jason said. "I don't think you'll want to ride your bike. But I'll be glad to give you a ride on mine. I brought an extra helmet. Is that okay?"

"Well . . . do you think you can bring me back here to get my bike later?"

"Sure."

"Okay, then."

Just like that, a person could turn her life around and climb on a motorcycle. Just like that a girl could reverse the direction of her life and go up a mountain to see what she'd find there. I was surprised and delighted at my own bravery. I wondered if it were true, as Franny had said, that Buddhists couldn't really fall in love. I hoped it wasn't true. Because Jason was special. Jason was beautiful.

Thirteen

Katya waved good-bye to us. The vision that stayed with me was the sun on her fair hair, her hand raised in farewell, and a look of wonder on her face. I knew what she was thinking: *Rachel Kaminsky on a motorcycle?* I knew how she felt — I never would have believed it myself.

My arms were around Jason, my cheek turned to rest against his back. I felt the weight of the helmet on my head, balanced there like an object of great beauty, like the baskets certain native women carried on their heads, filled with fruit or flowers or herbs. So much was coming at me at once — the feel of the wind against me as Jason accelerated, the buzz of the road beneath those big black wheels, the power of the machine vibrating through my entire body.

This must really be "living." It was not like living at the regular pace of life, but at some higher, more intense, level. This was the real thing. Finally!

Wind and sun and speed. Power and danger. My arms around a man. I felt light-headed and held on very tight.

"You okay?" Jason yelled over his shoulder.

"Fine," I called back, but the wind blew down my throat and made me choke. I closed my mouth tight.

We were on the same freeway my father usually took when we went to visit his sister, my Aunt Lily, or when we drove in winter to see the snow in the foothills near Mt. Baldy. But everything looked different — the car-wash places, the hamburger drive-ins, the mini-malls selling donuts and pizzas and wallpaper. It was all a matter of perspective.

When a person was in her father's station wagon, with her mother and her sisters, and she was going for a visit to Aunt Lily's, it was no wonder the world didn't look magical. But now — the donut signs looked like works of art, the banners flapping in the wind at the used-car lot looked like the flags of a great nation, and the shopping carts linked in a long line in front of the supermarket sparkled in the sun like a great silver necklace.

I closed my eyes and concentrated on the sensations. Jason took a curve, and I leaned with him into the wind. I felt as if we were figure skating together on the ice, leaning and banking and moving in perfect harmony. He lifted me, he launched me, I did a triple jump and landed like an angel. We were a pair of famous Russian skaters, we were world champions, we were . . .

"Hang on," Jason said. "We're heading straight up the mountain now."

These gardens invite the viewer to use the imagination to gain a more spiritual awareness of nature. The abstract forms symbolize features in nature. The slate walk represents a bank on the edge of a stream. A grove of ginkgo trees represents a forest carpeted with moss. Raked patterns in the gravel represent water flowing from a cascade formed by a tall stone and is backed by shrubbery suggesting low hills.

This garden can also be viewed as an impressionistic painting, the wall a canvas framed by black stones and cut granite. One should meditate on the scene and allow the imagination to be creative.

We were in a fantasy garden. There was no waterfall in front of me, but a rock over which I was supposed to imagine a cascade of water flowing. There were no flowers to be seen, but simply pebbles raked into gentle curves. Idea without substance was all around me, and a hush was in the air. I felt I was in a museum. Or maybe even a cemetery. Jason walked beside me, but his step was so light he seemed to float, ethereal, just above ground. Other guests visiting the monastery walked in silent appreciation around the imaginary garden.

When we came to a section of bonsai trees, I paused to read the little sign while Jason waited for me.

> *A bonsai is a tree maintained in dwarf form by methods limiting its growth. Even though only a foot tall, it can still have the features of a towering tree or a windswept pine clinging to a cliff.*

"Jason," I whispered, and he leaned down to catch my words. "Don't you think it's unfair to keep a tree from growing? To tie it up with wires so it achieves the shape you want from it?"

"It's a form of discipline, like all Zen discipline," Jason said. "It's a matter of control."

"But it's sort of like the old Chinese custom of binding women's feet, so they could have tiny, dainty feet." I stuck out my black Reeboks so Jason could see my feet, a healthy size 8. Big, strong, walking feet.

Jason smiled, but in his smile I saw that he knew I didn't understand the principle involved. Actually, I wasn't so sure I wanted to understand it. It didn't appeal to me very much.

"Shall we go in and sit *zazen*?"

"Can you tell me what it's like, exactly?"

"*Zazen* just helps you to still the useless rushing of your mind."

"My mind never feels useless, no matter what

85

it's doing." I felt I should tell him something about myself, because — although I would have liked to think he understood me completely — he didn't know me very well at all.

"Once you learn how useless it is, you'll want to calm your thoughts. But you can't expect to have results the first time. It takes a lot of practice to find that center, that quiet. But you can get a feel for it."

I thought about the feeling I'd had on the motorcycle, that center of physical sensation, that joy at being alive. I didn't know how Jason could do both: Could he really appreciate the roaring of his motorcycle, the noise and the passion of movement, and also love the silence of the Zen garden?

"Will they mind that I'm dressed all in black?" I asked him.

"Not at all. Black is a color that absorbs emotional electricity and leaves a clear field for meditation. The monks often wear black. Are you ready?"

"I'm ready," I said doubtfully. "Just don't expect too much of me. Okay?"

I had never flared my nostrils before. I had thought only horses could do that. Now I found, when instructed to do it, that I could do it quite well. My mouth had to be held closed, my teeth together but not clenched. The tip of my tongue was supposed to touch my lower teeth. And I had to be sure there was no air in my mouth.

This was "sitting *zazen*." Jason was beside me,

on his pillows, in the special posture we had been instructed to take. The pillows were very important, they had to be positioned exactly the right way. One of the teaching monks had shown us how to sit: in the lotus position, if we were flexible enough (cross-legged with each foot resting on the opposite thigh), or *seza*, sitting on the cushion in a kneeling position. That one was for beginners, or old folks. That was the position I was sitting in. Both my knees had to touch the floor.

The monk passing by us, in a long black robe, said, "Abdomen down, sternum up, ears, shoulders, and buttocks in line, nose above navel."

I knew I'd better not think too hard about my nose above my navel or I might burst out laughing. Jason had warned me that sometimes the monks went around hitting people lightly with little sticks if they made unacceptable body noises (swallowing, sniffling, yawning) or unacceptable body movements (blinking excessively, wiggling ears, and so forth).

The next thing I had to do was stare at the floor about three feet in front of me and make a *mudra*, a kind of cup, out of my hands, and hold them about two inches below my navel. That would turn out to be my *hara* — the center of gravity of the body, and a source of strength and stability.

It crossed my mind that if I wanted to do hard things with my body, I would rather become a great ice skater than a great meditator. Maybe I was just too young to sit still for so long.

"Keep your minds calm," the monk said. He was

very slender and nearly bald, and his voice was very soft. "Sitting *dhyana* will calm your minds," he told us.

I was getting thirsty. It was best not to get carried away with physical needs. I tried to come back to calmness and do the breathing discipline. We were supposed to breathe deeply — nostrils flared — very slowly.

"Be aware of your breathing but don't try to control it. Count to ten very slowly, and begin again. If a thought comes to your mind, let it rise and float away, but do not attach yourself to it or become involved with it."

Float — I thought of a root beer float. I thought of floating in a pool, stretched out on a silver raft, drinking iced tea. No, that was not the right approach. Scratch that one. Back to counting and breathing. I was aware of Jason's chest rising and falling in deep waves. He seemed still, and focused, all his attention inward. He didn't seem to be having thoughts like mine, thoughts like bubbles rising up in a root beer float. He didn't seem to be uncomfortable; as for me, my knee was hurting, and I was getting seriously bored.

Jason, Jason, I thought. *Are Buddhists allowed to have girlfriends?* I thought of all the men in my life — my father, Rick-my-little-boyfriend, Avram-the-rabbinical-student — and suddenly, out of nowhere, I thought of Karl, with his cheerful, ruddy, hanging-upside-down face. And I smiled involuntarily. Karl — he was going to bake bread this afternoon; he was hoping I'd come for dinner.

Stop thinking, I instructed myself. I flared my nostrils as wide as possible. I breathed. I tried not to blink. I let my thoughts float away, little white heart-shaped rings. And then, to my everlasting gratitude, a gong was rung — a great metallic gong — signifying the end of *zazen*. Now we were supposed to have a very brief vegetarian meal of something Jason had warned me resembled seaweed.

The monk was walking among us, reciting a little saying:

> *"Meditate.*
> *Live purely.*
> *Be quiet.*
> *Do your work*
> *With mastery."*

Fourteen

On the ride down the mountain, the taste of the strange, dark green, boiled vegetables still in my mouth, I held tight to Jason and let the mountain get lower and flatten out to lowlands while he worked out the complications of the road. Curves and swerves and banking and braking — let the man do the hard work; I was exhausted from flaring my nostrils. I had no problem with letting him figure out how to get back to civilization.

Franny would be impatient with my trust in him to get me safely back to civilization; she would call that my "dark ages" mentality. If she were on his motorcycle — which she wouldn't be! — she would be watching the road from over his shoulder, making sure he took the right turns. She didn't believe in relinquishing responsibility to men. It so happened I still believed men should do certain hard things: Let men read maps, and let men fix motors, and let men understand plumbing — I had better things to do. I also believed that if I were going to be in love with a man he ought to be a little older and a little taller than me. Franny would say that was selling out — that men have manipulated women to think that's important, that it's all part of the calculated oppression by the dominate group of the subordinate group.

Jason was taller than me. Avram was taller than me. Even Rick had been a little taller than me, although half the time he had been weighed down to a nub by all the things he hung on himself — Walkman radios, and calculators, and cameras, and digital watches that played little tunes. Men were generally taller than women — it couldn't be helped.

I hung on to Jason. The motorcycle was not something I would want to own. But I didn't mind hanging on to a man who owned one. It was nice to hang on to a man, I couldn't help feeling that way. I decided Franny must be very lonely, never hanging on to anyone. Didn't she sometimes feel like giving up her vigilance and letting someone else carry the load for a while?

Then I thought of Erica, and the way she flopped onto Harlan. Well, that was excessive. She leaned on him, hung on him, nearly always sat on his lap when he was around. There must be a nice middle ground somewhere.

"You okay?" Jason called.

"Fine," I yelled back. Talk was impossible. There was something nice about not having to have conversation. In the Zen gardens we couldn't talk, sitting *zazen* we couldn't talk, and on the motorcycle we couldn't talk. It we kept that up, we'd never disappoint each other!

When Jason pulled up to the curb in front of The Bargain Buggy, even after he'd turned off the ignition, my teeth continued to vibrate, and my skin felt as if electric shocks were passing through it.

"Wow," I said, unlocking my arms from Jason. "Wow." I climbed off the black leather seat, feeling very weak.

"Some baby, this machine," he agreed, smiling.

I walked a little erratically toward where my bicycle was still chained — it looked like a skinny, pitiful thing next to his bike. "Thanks a lot," I said. "It was a great day. It was — well, very interesting."

He looked pleased. "Great food, wasn't it?"

"Well — maybe you have to develop a taste for it," I admitted. I kept thinking I had green seaweed stuck between my teeth.

"It's a big battle," Jason said, "but it's worth it."

"What's a battle?"

"Giving up all worldly desires," he said. "That's

what screws us up. Aspiring. Wanting. Needing."

I had the feeling we shouldn't start talking and ruin everything, but my mouth was open before I could stop it.

"I'm young," I said. "I'm just *starting* to aspire."

"Nip it in the bud," Jason said. "Don't let it get you."

I aspire to see you again, I thought. So I said, "Do you want to meet me in The Bargain Buggy next Saturday? Maybe we could ride to the beach or somewhere." I had a sudden inspiration. "Or go ice skating!"

"Maybe," Jason said. "I never know where my spirit will lead me."

"I guess you don't like to be pinned down," I said, suddenly understanding a basic aspect of his nature. I also felt hurt, as if he'd insulted me.

"It's true, I'm sort of like a butterfly," he said. "I don't land in one place for long."

"But you wanted me to meet you here today," I said.

"Yes, I did. I could tell as soon as we met that you had a good spirit. I loved your black clothes," he said. "I thought you ought to see there's a different way to live, since you're sort of onto it already yourself. I wanted to show you the way of Zen."

"I thought you liked me for myself," I said. "But don't you think that if a person is onto finding a way to live that's best for her, she ought to keep on her own track?"

"There's no harm in someone showing you their

way," Jason said. He smiled, to show me there was no pressure he was putting on me. The smile felt like pressure.

"So I guess we'll only meet in Zen gardens in the future." I put it right on the line.

"Oh, no, not really. Look, Rachel," he said, "let's meet here again next weekend. We'll figure out where to take it from there. I do want to see you again. There *are* still things I want," he said. "It's just that I wish I didn't."

Was he implying that he wanted me and wished he didn't? The whole idea made me uncomfortable. I was out of my depth, talking this way. He was standing there, very tall and handsome, talking about strange secrets.

"Well, off I go to practice my breathing," I said, wanting to get back to the concrete, to stuff that made sense.

"So will you meet me here next week?" Now he was asking me very specifically.

"Maybe," I said. "Who knows? You can't pin a butterfly down." I grinned and got on my little bike and pointed it toward home. "I'll think about it. Good-bye, Jason," I said. "Live purely." I waved and pedaled away.

"Still want me to come over for dinner?" I asked Katya on the phone the minute I got home.

"Sure. What was it like? Did you like the bike? Were you afraid? Was it scary? Did he . . . ?"

"I'll tell you later," I said. "What's that weird noise I hear?"

"It's my brother, Karl. He's smashing the bread dough over and over."

"With a hammer or what?"

"With his fists. He's very vigorous," Katya said. "That's his style. So when will you get here?"

"I need to jump into the shower, but I'll be over soon."

My mother and sister had spent the day in the Bridal Shop of Bullock's Department Store. Erica was bent over the kitchen table studying a brochure of bridal veils.

"We picked out her crystal and silver patterns; what a huge job *that* was," Mom said proudly, as if they had solved a major problem of life.

"What patterns?" I asked. I was gulping down a can of root beer. Root beer had figured so passionately in my thirst fantasy at the monastery that I had to have one at the earliest moment possible.

"Sweet Paradise for my silverware," Erica said, "and Love's Eternal Etching for my crystal."

"Love's Eternal Itching?" asked Franny, who had padded into the kitchen in her bare feet.

Erica threw her a disgusted look.

"Speak not whereof you know nothing," my mother cautioned her. "Silver and crystal are essential household items when you set up house."

"How often do you use yours, Mom?" Franny asked, slyly. She tossed a lock of damp hair back over her shoulder. She opened the refrigerator and took out a big red apple, washed it, and bit into it.

"I'd use my silver service if I had a maid to help

me polish the silver," my mother said. "Or if you girls would help me . . . but unfortunately you don't seem able to find the time."

"Will Erica have a maid?" Franny asked innocently. "I thought Harlan wasn't quite a millionaire yet."

"Cool it," Erica said. "Don't spoil my day, Franny. You have no idea how many patterns there were to choose from — modern or classic, floral or sculpted, three-pronged or four-pronged forks, round or oval soupspoons."

"Sorry," Franny said. "I wasn't aware of the complexities a housewife has to deal with in serving soup."

Standing on tiptoe, she flung open a high cabinet in the kitchen and said to Mom, "Why don't you just give Erica your crystal? See all those glasses up there, the ones covered with dust? I don't think you've used them since . . . Mom, I don't think you've *ever* used those glasses!"

"Erica and I have discussed her taking them. Erica says she wants to choose her own. I may save them for Rachel."

"*For me?*" I could just see myself going off to The Mountainside School, my backpack stuffed with long-stemmed crystal.

"Tomorrow we're going to buy my wedding dress," Erica said. She said it as if it were the sentence she'd been waiting all her life to say. She said it as if it were poetry.

"But," my mother said, "it's such a pity to wear a gorgeous new wedding dress in the dirt and grass! I wish you and Harlan would reconsider your plans to get married up on some weedy mountain. Why not a nice, clean hotel, with a nice ballroom, and nice *hors d'oeuvres* served on nice silver trays?''

Erica's lips tightened. I was pleased to see she was able to draw the line somewhere. ''That's what Harlan wants, Mother. We've made our decision to say our vows under tall pine trees. Harlan's had that dream for years.''

''And remember,'' Franny reminded my mother, ''that's a *computer programmer's* mind.''

''Still,'' Mom said, ''there could be bees, there could be mosquitoes.''

''We'll take our vows under the glorious canopy of God's blue heaven,'' Erica said. I think she was quoting Harlan — it didn't sound like her.

''And you,'' Mom said, turning to me. ''You'll come with us tomorrow and buy a dress for the wedding!''

''Me? A dress?'' My voice cracked.

''Something summery and cool, a dotted Swiss, or an organdy, something pastel.''

''Pastel? Mom,'' Franny said, ''have you noticed that Rachel isn't into pastels lately? Or did you happen to miss that phenomenon?''

''And you,'' my mother said, turning on Franny. ''You're not immune to this, either. You can't attend a wedding in cutoff shorts. No, there are limits! If you and Rachel are members of this family and plan to attend the wedding, you will have to dress appropriately.''

''I'll find something,'' Franny said breezily. ''I won't humiliate any of you.''

''But you,'' Mom turned back to me. ''You cannot wear black to this event. This is a wedding, not a funeral."

"I'll think about it," I said. The last thing I wanted was to have my mother drag me to Bullock's on Sunday. Why didn't department stores close on Sunday, anyway?

"Oh, but I can't go shopping tomorrow!" I announced suddenly — how lucky that I had remembered. "I just remembered that I'm going to an Orthodox Jewish wedding tomorrow. With Avram, the head counselor at camp. His cousin Yeheuda is getting married."

"An orthodox wedding? Heaven help the poor bride!" Franny said. "She'll have three babies in the next three years."

"A wedding," Erica said dreamily. "How wonderful. I feel like a sister to all brides these days. I wish I could come."

"A wedding!" Mom said. "And what do you plan to wear to it? Your black sneakers?"

Just then, Daddy popped in the back door; his yellow T-shirt had a chipmunk playing a harpsichord on it, with the words underneath: *GOPHER BAROQUE*.

"I'll wear Daddy's T-shirt," I said, inspired.

He blinked. Poor Dad. He didn't know what was going on — he almost never did.

Fifteen

"Come in, my dear," Mrs. Ohlendorf said. "My, what a handsome shirt that is. Such a good quality wool, and such a nice black dye they used on it."

I grinned my thanks. Mrs. Ohlendorf had been a seamstress in Germany; she was an expert on fine clothing, and she sometimes made Katya dresses with impressive hidden buttonholes, invisible hemstitching, elaborately embroidered collars. In Germany (Katya had told me) all women were trained to be excellent housekeepers. It occurred to me that it wasn't so different from what Orthodox Jewish wives were expected to be.

From the kitchen came the smell of baking bread, warm and sweet and delicious.

"Karl has been baking up a storm," Mrs. Ohlendorf explained to me. "That boy — he was covered with flour, on his hair, on his eyebrows, all over his shirt. I made him go and change. I said, you can't receive a young lady in this condition!"

She laughed, and I laughed with her. I really liked Mrs. Ohlendorf. She always made me feel at home and comfortable. Even though her house was neat, it wasn't like a museum. When *my* mother got ready for company, she gave orders that no one was allowed to sit on the couch, no one was allowed to use the guest towels in the bathroom, no one should dare leave a cup in the sink. She turned into Mrs. Clean, the Monster Lady.

Katya came zooming into the living room, wearing her red cape. The young people in this house didn't move in normal ways, but instead seemed jet-propelled.

She swirled around for us. "You know, I feel like some great lady, maybe royalty," she said. "I think we women got cheated, Rachel, being born in modern times. If we had lived in the olden days, we could have worn bustles and crinolines and hoops — like out of *Gone With the Wind*."

"Oh, you'd hate it, Katya," Mrs. Ohlendorf said, with a wave of her hand. She shook her head so that her crown of blonde hair shimmered. "All that fussing with ribbons and bows. You know how impatient you are! You know how you rip open the snaps on your jacket, and it's done. Or you pull the Velcro on your sneakers, and they're off!"

"But Velcro isn't glamorous," Katya said, giving another little swirl so that the cape flared out. "I vant to be glam — ooo — rus!"

"So try putting a lampshade over your head!" Karl appeared in the doorway and grabbed a cushion from a chair. He held it in front of Katya's face. "You really look much better this way," he said, turning toward me. "Doesn't she?"

"And you! You'd look better with a trash can over your head," Katya answered. He swatted her, and she began chasing him down the hall. Mrs. Ohlendorf turned her palms up.

"These children," she said. "Fighting all their lives like this?"

"But in fun," I said. "It looks like fun to me."

"Sometimes in fun. Sometimes their fights are not so funny." She shrugged. "But what can a mother do? Go and cook dinner, yes?"

I nodded my agreement.

"Make yourself at home, Rachel. They'll be back in no time. This is a small house to chase through. So I will go and check on the dinner."

On the wall were some charcoal sketches I had never noticed before — two of them were of men who resembled uncles of mine. That is, they had features that were familiar to me — a certain slant of forehead, shape of nose, hairline. Sort of a cross between my grandfather and me. I could hear Katya and Karl still running through the house, laughing, horsing around.

Katya came racing in, breathless, her face red. "I could kill my brother," she said. "His mission in life is to drive me nuts."

Karl reappeared, flushed and panting, holding out a big bath towel. He dumped it over Katya's

101

head and said, "Now this is a very fine style of headware for you . . . it so flatters your features."

"Oh, you dummy, why don't you take a long walk off a short pier?"

"Enough," said a deep voice. "You give me a headache already!" Mr. Ohlendorf shuffled into the living room. He always wore a hat because, Katya had told me, he hated his bald head. But he wore interesting hats — baseball caps and berets, stocking caps and little beanies. Today he wore his beret. He still had a deep German accent, and sometimes it was hard for me to understand everything he said.

"Gertrude — " he called into the kitchen, "little Rachel here is starving for dinner. So where is her dinner?"

"I'm fine, Mr. Ohlendorf, I'm not starving."

"No," Katya said, "she had a huge lunch at a monastery this afternoon."

"This is true?" Mr. Ohlendorf asked me. "What monastery?"

"Oh, it's a Zen Center on Mt. Baldy." I hoped he wasn't sensitive to the word "bald" in any form. "I ate some kind of seaweed there for lunch," I said. "A friend wanted me to see the place, and they have an open house for guests every Saturday."

"Seaweed? I think you will find that Gertrude will do better than that tonight."

"And with Karl's bread," Mrs. Ohlendorf said, wiping her hands on her apron and motioning us into the kitchen. "The best of the best."

"Shall we eat then?" Karl said.

102

"After you?" Mr. Ohlendorf said to his wife.

"After you," Karl said to me. He bowed like a true gentleman, and I laughed. "Or how about we get there at the same time so no one gets a head start on the roast?"

Karl crooked his arm through mine and escorted me into dinner.

The roast beef and baked potatoes were delicious; the bread was set down on a silver platter, crusty and golden. Mrs. Ohlendorf had used a butter press so that our bread and butter plates each contained a glistening slab of butter with the impression of a rose on it. She had set the table with linen napkins and heavy silverware; I thought it looked elegant. When it occurred to me that my sister Erica aspired to a home like this, something went *clunk* in my mind. It didn't seem to me that Erica and Harlan could ever carry it off the way the Ohlendorfs did. Maybe it was the Ohlendorfs' European heritage! But it seemed to be something else, a sense of style and grace, something that you couldn't get just by registering your china and silver patterns at the local department store.

"Taste this," Karl said to me. He tore off a chunk of bread and buttered it for me. He held it to my lips while I took a bite.

"Oh, that's wonderful," I sighed. The inside was soft and delicate; the crust was amazing.

"Good bread, yes," Mr. Ohlendorf said, "but tuition at the baker's college — that makes every loaf of bread Karl bakes cost maybe fifty dollars!"

"Oh, you," Mrs. Ohlendorf said to him. "The

boy will earn a good living soon. It's worth every penny, to teach him to be a master baker."

"My father learned it without fancy colleges," Mr. Ohlendorf said. "It's in the genes."

"Good genes *and* education — they make a better batter," Mrs. Ohlendorf suggested.

"Are any of those men in the sketches in the living room," I asked, "are any of them your father?"

"Oh, no," Mr. Ohlendorf said. "Those are poor dead Jews. Poor fellows, the Nazis killed them. The sketches were done by a Jewish opera singer who was also killed by the Nazis."

I felt my throat close — I didn't know what to say. I didn't know what to *think*.

Mrs. Ohlendorf reached over and touched my arm. "Dieter," she said to Mr. Ohlendorf. "Explain to the child after you said such a shocking thing."

"What can I say?" Mr. Ohlendorf said. "The artist who did those drawings was a friend of my family's — he was also an opera singer. He drew the faces of his Jewish friends. When the Nazis arrested him, these drawings were left behind. Then, after the war, his children found them and gave them to my family because they knew my father and the opera singer had been good friends. And so they are in our house now, a memorial to those poor people."

A thousand questions came to my mind, but I asked none of them. The Ohlendorfs had known Jews and knew of Nazis who had killed them; they had been in Germany during the terrible time of the war. If they had had Jewish friends, I was sure

104

they couldn't have been conspirators against the Jews. But I thought of what Avram would say. He had already *said* to me in one of our talks that many Germans pretended they didn't know what was going on when they really had. How could they *not* know, he had demanded of me, when thousands of their countrymen were being taken away daily to be killed?

I ate my bread and butter. I finished my roast and potatoes. Mrs. Ohlendorf served plum cake for dessert, with sweet tea.

After dinner, Mr. Ohlendorf put on a record of German folk songs and Katya sank down on the couch with a magazine. Up on the wall were the drawings of the Jewish people killed by the Nazis. The men could have been my uncles. My *father*. Like the fate of Anne Frank, their fate was almost too terrible to think about.

I felt shivery in the presence of all this history, and in my awareness that I was in the home of *Germans*. But I consoled myself that the war was over. That time had passed. That was then; this was now. I knew Avram would say it could never pass, that we must never forget. And I knew no one *should* ever forget. But the Ohlendorfs were our neighbors, and Katya was my friend. We were all Americans, and we had just eaten a fine dinner together. Music was playing. I didn't want to hate, and I didn't want to blame the Ohlendorfs!

Sixteen

Somehow it had gotten late. The dinner dishes were washed and put away, the counters were shining and clear. Down the hall, we could hear Mrs. Ohlendorf's sewing machine clicking away. Mr. Ohlendorf had gone into his bedroom to watch television, and Katya had fallen asleep reading on the couch. Karl had offered to teach me how to make *challah*, after I'd confided to him how my mother had faked my camp application, certain that I'd never "blow my own horn" but wanting to be sure I got the job.

Unlike Avram, who thought what my mother

had done was dishonorable, Karl thought it was funny, "a kick."

"I wouldn't say it was cheating," Karl said, "not if you really bone up on origami and all that stuff you're supposed to know. The way I see it is that you already know more than the camp kids know on just about every subject. And what you don't know you can find out, right? So would you like me to teach you how to bake *challah*, right now?"

"Would you, really? I'm actually in charge of *challah*-making at camp next week. I've already read the recipe in the cookbook ten times, but it's not the same as having practiced it."

"No problem — just throw this apron over your head," Karl said. "If you get white flour all over your black wool shirt, you'll be quite a sight. We could both end up looking like ghouls." He tossed me an apron that had printed on it, "Kissin' Don't Last, Cookin' Do."

"Is this some kind of philosophical truth?" I asked him.

"We may have to try it out," he said, "and see for ourselves."

Then he took on a businesslike tone. "First we put a package of yeast, two teaspoons of sugar, and a quarter cup of warm water in a bowl and let it stand five minutes." Karl swept around his mother's kitchen, reaching here and there with his long, angular arms to grab a bowl, a measuring cup, a mixing spoon. His movements were loose and relaxed; I had never seen him when he didn't seem to be enjoying himself. He loved to talk about

107

things he cared about, but, unlike Avram, or even Jason, he didn't take himself so seriously. He didn't "preach" to me.

Also, he made me laugh a lot, which was a great relief after being with my other serious men-friends. He kicked off his shoes, jumped up on the table (wearing the cleanest white socks I'd ever seen), and unscrewed one of the two light bulbs in the ceiling fixture.

"What on earth are you doing?"

"It's good for the dough. No one wants to expand and develop under glaring lights. Would you want to?"

"Would I want to expand and develop?" Deciding not to risk a comment Karl might take in the wrong way, I changed the subject. "It is much nicer in the dimness, just in general. It's sort of like my darkroom when I have the safelight on. All things seem possible then. I get very peaceful there."

"Baking bread gives me that feeling, too," Karl said. "I feel like I'm in touch with a kind of essential act. Bread is the staff of life, you know. The most basic food on earth. It's a kind of holy thing to do — mix up some dry stuff with some wet stuff, and out comes this amazing loaf of bread."

"Do you know the story about matzos?" I asked him.

"Tell me," he said.

"Well, when the Jews were fleeing Egypt they didn't have time to let the bread rise, so they had to bake unleavened bread. That's why Jews have to eat matzo during Passover. It's the flat bread that reminds us of what the Jews had to endure."

"Do you have Passover seders at your house?"

"No, not really, we're only sort-of very mildly religious. I guess no one has ever been very serious about it in my house, and that makes my father feel guilty. He's always felt it's his duty to get us to be truly religious, and since he hasn't, he feels he's failed us in some way. Once or twice he tried to do the whole ritual — you know, the prayers, the story of the Exodus, the glass of wine for the prophet Elijah, the hard-boiled egg, and the bitter herbs — but when we actually sat down at the table, Franny started giggling, and Erica got restless, and my mother said the meat was getting overcooked — and we just didn't have the patience for the whole thing."

"Religion takes a *lot* of patience," Karl said. "You have to have the right temperament to be religious."

"Do you have it?"

"I believe in yeast," Karl said. "In its special and marvelous powers. I believe in bread."

He went to work making the dough while I watched. He sifted the flour and salt into a bowl. He made a well in the center of the dry ingredients and dropped in the eggs, some oil, and the yeast mixture.

"Here we go," he said. "Here's where a man's real muscle power counts." He began to knead the dough on a floured cutting board.

I leaned against the kitchen cabinets and watched him work, watched his muscles flex, watched the rhythm of his back as he leaned into the dough and pressed, released, doubled the dough over, and kneaded it again. His hands were very strong. Just watching them made me weak-kneed.

After a time he looked up at me, with surprise, as if he had forgotten me. "You know, there's this perfect moment when you have to stop," he said, " — when everything is mixed just right, and it's time to let the magic do its work."

Gently, very gently, he placed the dough in a bowl and brushed the top of it with a little oil. Then, as if he were covering a beloved child at bedtime, he covered the dough with a dish towel and placed the bowl on the stove, over the pilot light.

"We have to let it rise in a warm place for about an hour," he said.

"An hour? And then we have to bake it? You know, it's really getting late, Karl. I have to go home before my parents have a fit."

"Call your folks. Tell them you're baking *challah*. They can't object to that."

"No, they can't," I agreed. "Between my father and my mother they're bound to approve of something that's both Jewish and domestic in nature." I smiled at Karl. He patted my apron in a neutral place — across the words "Kissin' Don't Last," and a puff of white flour rose in the air like a burst of stars.

"You know where the phone is," he said. "Call them."

While we waited for the dough to rise, Karl put some music on the stereo and then sat down in an armchair, tapping his feet to the rhythm. Katya woke up, dazed, and mumbled that she didn't want to interrupt her dream. She waved to us and stumbled off to bed. In a short time, the sewing machine stopped clicking and became quiet. Mrs. Ohlendorf stuck her head into the living room and said good night to us.

"Want to dance with me?" Karl asked.

"Won't we disturb everyone?"

"Oh, no, I always dance at midnight," he said. "My folks won't notice, so think nothing of it." He stood and held out his arms to me.

The music was so inviting, the beat so compelling, I couldn't resist. I came into his arms, and we moved slowly over the polished wood of the living room floor. I leaned my cheek against the hard roundness of his shoulder, smelling his scent of powder and shaving lotion. When the slow dance ended, something loud came on, and Karl clicked it off. He led me to the couch, where we both sat for a moment without talking.

"You're a very great girl," Karl said, finally, to me. "Very great, indeed."

"Thank you," I said. "Thank you very much."

"My sister is lucky to have you for a friend."

"She's lucky to have you for a brother. I have only sisters, you know."

"You could adopt me to be your brother," Karl said. He had an impish look on his face. "But of course, if we fell in love then it would be a problem."

"Silly," I said.

"It could happen," he said. "Worse things have been known to happen."

"Karl," I said. "Do you realize that we're almost natural enemies, a German and a Jew?"

"You don't believe that, do you?" Karl asked. "Do you really think you and I are natural enemies of some sort?"

"I know someone who says we have to be. He's going to be a rabbi."

"But he's wrong," Karl said. "He wants to perpetuate hate. Is that any way to live? Especially if he's a religious man? Do you think religion ought to be a basis for hate? 'Unite and hate,' that's our motto?"

"I hate to hate," I said simply. "It's a rotten feeling, and it doesn't make sense to me."

"Then don't hate," he said simply. "Love instead."

"Love who?"

"Love everyone. Love me," Karl said. He kissed me very suddenly on my cheek. "We can start out with very benign, friendly love. Then we can advance it into deeper, more . . . serious stuff."

"If you kiss me again," I said, "please make it very friendly. I'm not ready for the serious love yet."

"Then we can take our time," Karl assured me. "We're both young, we have plenty of time."

He kissed me again, this time on the lips. But it was light, it was friendly. I could taste a faint powdering of flour afterward. He seemed to think we should try another kiss.

"Do you think the dough has risen yet?" I suggested.

"Well, who knows? But let's go see." He pulled me up from the couch, and we went into the kitchen to stand over the warmth of the stove. Karl lifted the edge of the towel, and we witnessed the amazing change that had occurred; the little, dense, hard lump of kneaded dough was now risen like a white moon. Its surface was gently ridged and shining with oil.

"Punch it down," Karl said. "Go ahead, and then we'll make three strands and braid the *challah*."

"Punch it?"

"It's not violence in this context," Karl said. "It's tenderness and love. Go ahead," he urged me. "I give you permission to punch." So I punched the warm dough with my fist, happily, joyfully.

Seventeen

Yeheuda's groom was named Shlomo. As we drove to the synagogue on Sunday morning, Avram told me they were going to move to Israel after the wedding and devote their lives to God.

"That's interesting," I said. I could hardly believe the irreverent thought that flew through my mind; of course, I couldn't reveal it to Avram. I would have liked to ask him why people would devote their lives to God (who was pretty well-equipped to fend for Himself) when there was so much work to be done on earth for human beings. I had this irreverent strain of practicality in me — it always popped out and shocked people. I knew Avram wouldn't appreciate it. It was a major strain being with someone to whom you were afraid to speak your mind.

I was dressed to the point of suffocation. Not a square inch of my skin was visible below my chin, above my wrists, or above my ankles. This morning Franny had loaned me a long black skirt; I had put on my own black cotton turtleneck. Franny had pulled out of her closet a Spanish black lace shawl (she had worn it in a production of *Blood Wedding* when she was in drama class in high school), and she covered my hair with it.

"You know, of course, that hair," she had said, "is just too erotic for orthodox men."

"I don't have erotic hair," I said, "I just have these wild curls."

"Curls is what drives 'em crazy," Franny said. "Think of these poor men who study all day, think of what they have to deal with. Their minds are on lofty subjects when suddenly they look up from their books and catch a glimpse of a woman with curls. The minute they see curls on a female, they run amuck!"

"Come on, Franny," I said. "Be more respectful. Just because we don't really understand someone's religion is no reason to make fun of it."

"I understand enough!" she said.

"But you and I haven't studied it deeply." I had come to that conclusion after my visit to the Zen monastery. It wasn't fair, I'd decided, to dismiss an entire way of life on the basis of a two-hour experience. The other thing I'd concluded was that I was pretty sure I didn't *want* more than a two-hour experience of it! Was that fair? But I had to trust myself *somewhere* along the line. If something felt wrong to me, I didn't see the point of pursuing it just to convince myself that maybe, eventually, it would feel right!

I admired my covered form in Franny's mirror. "I look sort of Arabic," I said, draping the black shawl under my eyes. "I could almost be one of those mysterious Muslim women who aren't allowed to show their faces. Maybe I could fool everyone into thinking I was really beautiful."

"You're not the type," Franny said.

"I know," I said mournfully. "I'll never be beautiful."

"NO!" Franny said. "You are beautiful, Rachel. That's not what I meant. You're not the type to live your life under a shawl. You're a free spirit."

I was separated from Avram at the door of the synagogue and sent by a man in a black hat to sit in an upstairs balcony with other women. I looked at Avram beseechingly as I was directed up the stairs, but he didn't even wave. He went directly — his eyes held straight ahead — into the downstairs chapel, where I could see a bunch of other bearded, black-coated men. So much for attending this wedding with Avram, so much for being at his side while we watched two lovers join their hearts for all eternity.

Upstairs the benches had filled up with women,

some of them quite young, nearly all of them wearing scarves on their heads. The women were chattering and talking animatedly to one another, as if many of them were old and good friends.

The young woman who was sitting beside me turned to me and smiled. "Are you from Shlomo's family?"

"I'm from Song of Solomon," I said, and then felt like an idiot. I was beginning to sweat in my black outfit, which by now was feeling like ski coveralls. I glanced down over the railing. Nothing was happening down on the lower level, so I stood up, said "Excuse me" to the women I had to pass by, and made my way out to the aisle and to freedom. I had to have a drink of water!

I went down the stairs and tiptoed nervously along a narrow corridor. I could find no door that was marked Ladies Room. Maybe the Orthodox didn't believe in marking doors. Maybe they had a *law* against writing on doors. But I was getting really desperate; thinking there had to be water somewhere, I very cautiously opened a door.

Behind it I found the bride! She was sitting alone in a room, on a chair, stiff as a doll. When she heard me enter, she didn't move her head, only swerved her eyes in my direction. She was dressed in a white satin gown, her head and face covered by a long lace veil. Her eyes — distant-looking behind the veil — watched me with vague interest. She didn't speak. Behind her, on a little card table, was a bouquet of yellow flowers.

"Excuse me," I whispered. "I'm just a little lost.

117

I was trying to find a ladies room."

She nodded, almost trancelike.

"I know you're Avram's cousin. I work at the day camp with him."

She nodded again.

"I guess you're waiting for everything to happen," I suggested lamely, not knowing what else to say.

The sound of her voice shocked me. She said: "He has to decide. He's doing it now."

"Decide what? Do you mean that right now he's deciding if he should marry you?"

She nodded.

"Don't *you* have to do any deciding?"

"Oh, no," she said. "He is being advised by the rabbis and his friends. This is a very important decision for him, you know."

"And not for you?"

She didn't answer.

"Well — " What else was there to say? "Good luck and everything. Have a wonderful wedding." I waved, but she had straightened her shoulders and seemed to be staring at the far wall. I went out of the room and left her there in the silence.

I saw another room and tried the doorknob. The door swung inward and suddenly it was as if I had entered a chicken coop. There was such a babbling going on it took my breath away. The room was full of men in black suits, black hats, and black beards. They were addressing one another and arguing in loud voices. They seemed to be directing their comments toward a young man seated at the head of a long table. He wore an elaborately embroidered *yarmulke* and was studying a document he held in one hand. In the other hand he held a long black fountain pen.

Whenever one of the men shouted something to him, he nodded his head five or ten times. He kept putting the tip of the pen to the paper, as if to write on it, and then lifted it away as he listened to someone else's commentary.

Suddenly one of the men looked up and saw me. He made a sound like a hen that had been stepped on. "Go! Go! Go!" he cried, shooing me away. "No women in here!" At that instant I recognized Rabbi Gelber, from our own day camp! He saw me at the same moment, and I thanked heaven that he recognized me. He quickly took my arm and led me into the hallway.

"I'm sorry, my dear — what is your name again?"

"Rachel Kaminsky."

"Yes, well, Rachel — this part of the wedding is for the men only."

"What's going on?" I asked him.

"The groom has to sign the writ of marriage, accepting the woman as his bride. Since their betrothal he has been thinking it over carefully. Now is the moment when he makes his final decision, to accept her or reject her."

"At *this* late date?" I asked in astonishment.

"It's just a part of our tradition," Rabbi Gelber said. "I wouldn't worry. The groom rarely refuses her at this moment."

"And then the bride has to sign the agreement?" I asked, just for the sake of asking, but knowing the answer.

"No, she signs nothing," he said. "It is only for him to decide if he wants her. He and the other men are judging her qualities before the two of them become irrevocably joined."

"What if he turns her down?" I insisted. I imagined I would be given the job to go in the next room and tell Yeheuda that it was all off, that Shlomo had jilted her at the last minute because he had found out she couldn't make *challah*. "Don't you think she ought to discuss *his* qualities with her friends, too?"

Rabbi Gelber looked at me with his patient gaze. "I'm sure she has, my dear," he said. "And I'm sure that in their married life together, she will be equal to him . . . or more so! But in these matters of ritual, which have been conducted for centuries in a certain way, the Orthodox observe the ancient customs."

"But if this were a modern Jewish wedding . . ." I began.

"If this were a Reform wedding, or a Conservative wedding," Rabbi Gelber assured me, "you would find the customs had been adjusted to serve the times. Remember, my dear, that only the Orthodox stick hard and fast to the old ways."

"I think they're too hard for me," I said.

Just then a woman in a yellow dress came down the hall carrying a large dinner plate. She entered the room where the men were still babbling.

"How come she can go in?" I asked. "*She's* a woman."

"She's the mother of the bride. She's been given word that the groom has signed, and now she has to go in there and break a plate."

"Rabbi Gelber," I said. "I have only one more simple question to ask you. Do you think there's a water fountain around here somewhere?"

Eighteen

The *chupah*, the canopy under which the bride and groom stood during the ceremony, was made of red silk with a gold fringe. Looking down from the balcony with the other women, I could see the hats of the eight rabbis who were officiating at the service. Shlomo wore a long white robe. Yeheuda, under her veil, stood head bowed, as Shlomo and the eight rabbis did what had to be done. The service was entirely in Hebrew, and I understood none of it.

At one point, Yeheuda's mother took her daughter's hand and together they circled the groom seven times. As they went round and round, I began to feel dizzy myself. I knew this was an important moment in an important ritual. I knew I didn't properly understand it. But still, I felt deeply uncomfortable, as if I weren't watching the rites of a marriage between people of my own religion, and of nearly my own age. One of them was the cousin of Avram, a man who I thought was, in some ways, deeply attractive and who I — in my fantasies — could almost imagine (possibly) marrying!

But that fantasy was being dashed to bits. I prided myself on not making flash judgments, but I thought of Yeheuda sitting alone in that empty room, while the groom and his buddies were deciding if the marriage was going to go on or not, and I thought: *Not for me! No indeed. Not for me!*

When the service was finally over, the bride and groom did not kiss, but were pulled apart and were hugged by members of their families.

The women near me in the balcony all rose and began to move toward the stairs. I went down with them and saw crowds convening in the banquet hall, but the bride and groom were not among them.

I stepped over to a woman with a baby on her hip and asked her where the newlyweds were.

"They have to take some time alone together now," she explained, looking at me as if I were incredibly dense.

"To get to know each other?" I asked. But she had moved off to gather with some other women at a table, and I found myself looking for Avram. I finally spotted him at a table, talking with some

123

bearded men. I wasn't even sure it was Avram. Somehow the men looked generic to me — all from the same mold, bearing the same shape, dress, and manner.

I started to walk toward him and then realized that *none* of the men and women were mingling. The women were taking places together at round tables on one side of the room, and the men were gathering at tables across the floor.

I didn't know anyone here, and being at a party all alone was not quite the idea I had had in mind.

I heard a blast of music and looked up to see that one of the eight rabbis (I was *pretty* sure he was one of them), the one with the fullest, blackest beard, had begun to play a trumpet solo at the front of the room. Soon a five-piece band joined in and the dancing began. Dancing! Men with men, and women with women! This had been the custom in the town of Anatevka in Russia in *Fiddler on the Roof* — but in *California* at the end of the *twentieth century?*

I took a seat and just watched. There was no lack of energy and joy. The music was loud, and the men dancing seemed to enjoy stamping their feet. A woman with her hair covered by a blue silk scarf said, "Aah, there is Shlomo." I saw the groom come in, once again in his black suit.

"Where is his white robe?" I asked the woman in the blue scarf.

"His white robe? That's his shroud," she said. "He won't wear that again till he dies, and then he'll be buried in it."

"Oh, I see," I said. *I didn't see.* What did all this

mean? I was alarmed to feel myself so alienated and doubting. I felt I was rooted in another world, another century, as if I had stepped into a time machine that took me back two hundred years to visit the past.

The groom and one of the men had begun to dance together. They started slowly, and began to circle around, kicking and jumping with tremendous passion and energy. I could feel the floor shake with each thump of their powerful legs. Other bearded men took their hands; they pulled one another, faster and faster, around in a widening circle. The groom was expressionless, yet his red face and his wild dancing convinced me he was having an intense experience.

I heard a collective gasp from the women and I turned toward the doorway where Yeheuda had just entered. She stood like an angel, her veil turned back so that her pale face was visible. She smiled.

The women moved in a wave toward her and absorbed her into their midst. A moment later they had opened up, like a colorful flower, with her in their center, and had begun to dance around her. A chair was brought forth, and they sat her on it and lifted it, Yeheuda trembling precariously, but blushing and smiling, high above them. Enthroned there, she glowed with joy. I felt sad. I felt lonely and excluded, aware that I would never be a queen like that, even for one minute of my life.

But would you want to be? Franny's voice said in my ear. *Yes. Maybe. Who knows? Why not?* some part of me answered.

Now, as if by plan, the groom was also placed in a chair and hoisted high in the air by the men, and the lines of men and women carried the wedded pair on their chairs toward one another where they stared into each other's eyes over the heads of the others. I looked away. I felt as if I had intruded into their privacy. I didn't feel I had earned the right to see this.

I saw that most of the women, many of them not much older than I was, wore gold wedding bands. A few had small babies with them. They seemed animated and joyful. They all looked beautiful to me. One, wearing a tasseled rope tied low around her waist, began to do a dance, shimmying — and making a hooting sound by waving her hand over her lips. It seemed to be a message to the bride.

I wondered if I would ever belong to a community of people who shared the same values and goals I did. I wasn't even sure yet what my values and goals were.

I tried to find Avram again and discovered that he was in the center of the dance floor, trying to balance a bottle on his head while dancing the *kasatski*. I knew *that* dance. I had seen it done in the wedding scene in *Fiddler on the Roof*.

The words of the matchmaker song from *Fiddler on the Roof* came back to me again:

> *For Papa, make him a scholar,*
> *For Mama, make him rich as a king,*
> *For me, well, I wouldn't holler*
> *If he were as handsome as anything!*

I wasn't like the girl singing that song. Maybe it was a fatal flaw in my nature, but I knew I wasn't going to be all that concerned with what my mother and father wanted. I knew I wouldn't marry anyone for qualities my mother or my father (or anyone else) wanted a husband of mine to have. It would kill me if I felt I should marry early for *Erica's sake*, or not marry at all for *Franny's*. I had to figure out what was best for *my* sake. And when on earth would I be able to do that? When would I know I was ready to decide what was best for *me*? And what if I *never* knew?

Some woman passed by me holding a tray on which little plastic goblets of red wine were filled to the brim, shimmering.

I took one and thanked her. All around me people held up their glasses, ready to toast the bride and groom. I toasted them and sipped the sweet wine, making a little toast to myself as well:

> *To Rachel and to her future:*
> *May she someday find her beloved.*
> *May he be* handsome as anything
> *and also suitable in every other way!*

Nineteen

The Mountainside School promised in their booklet that relationships among their students were based on *real mutual interests outside the artificial boundaries of age groupings, pairing-off difficulties, and other unconscious feelings and identifications that promote cliques and exclusive groups.*

I tried to picture myself living on a bus for a whole school year. I'd have to plan meals and cook. I'd be able to shower only occasionally, when the bus was at a campsite with hot running water. Some nights we'd be sleeping on rocks and other nights on soft pine-covered surfaces. There would be bugs — lots of them, big mean ones and little nasty ones. And of course there would be birds — the sky would be filled with birds — eagles and hawks and doves and sparrows.

My heart thrilled at the thought of what might pass across the lenses of my binoculars. And stars, there would be stars at night, brilliant in the pitch-black heavens.

I tried to compare that vision to what I knew of regular high school — the usual locked-in feeling of waiting for the bell to ring, the endless chatter of teachers, the parties and dances you hoped you'd go to but usually didn't get asked to, the daily friction with parents. *When will you be home? Who will you be going with? Why do you have to go? How come you're not studying?* I didn't even look forward to the privileges of being a senior. "Senior ditch day" was only one day out of the classroom, whereas The Mountainside School would offer a full school year in the country, in the fresh air, in the mountains, and beside streams. We'd study ecology, biology, botany, animal behavior, astronomy, geology. We'd have field trips to study, first-hand, archaeology and anthropology. We would learn music and folklore, geography, home economics, earth science, and the psychology of group dynamics. And the English class, instead of being the usual grammar and composition, would offer a chance to "write your own autobiography."

The whole program sounded immensely exciting to me — the books and studying would be mixed with discovery and action. Recently, these days when I had so much unfocused energy, I felt what I needed most was action.

129

The Mountainside School was fully accredited, which meant getting into college wouldn't be a problem. But would they pick me?

I only hoped the essay in my application hadn't been too stupid. What had I said, exactly? Something earnest about how I had loved animals all my life, that I raised birds and appreciated nature. Now I was embarrassed that I had actually said that my goal in life was to "delve into the secrets of nature." I had gone on in this vein to say how important it was to me to "relate to the spirit of this great planet Earth we live on." Well, I had done the best I could do. Maybe a little excessive prose wouldn't be taken in the wrong way. I hoped they would understand my earnestness was sincere. (And maybe no one else had done any better.) Only time would tell. I wasn't going to find out if I was accepted till the middle of August. I just had to be patient . . . and pray. Maybe Avram would pray for me, since I wasn't very big on praying. Or maybe Jason could. But neither of them, it seemed to me, would have a direct line of communication to the headmaster of The Mountainside School. I would just have to wait and see.

Now that it was Saturday, I was planning to work in my darkroom. The week at camp had been weird; Avram hadn't actually ignored me, but he'd treated me very formally, as if he'd hoped the wedding would have convinced me to follow the orthodox life and now was disappointed that I hadn't been converted and made my pledge to him. But then again, formal behavior was his trademark;

130

maybe he was feeling just as friendly as always. Maybe his gaze was not one of disapproval but of consideration. Maybe he was wondering if I'd make a good wife for him!

The trouble was that I could never "read" Avram. Sometimes the kids at camp reacted the same way. They'd think he was angry or that he disapproved of something they were doing when, in fact, he was miles away, frowning at something in his head that had nothing to do with any of them.

There was a knock on my bedroom door. I tried a new tack.

"Who is it and *please don't come in*," I said.

My mother pushed open the door.

"Someone to see you," she said, "out front." Her face looked peculiar. "On a *vehicle*," she added.

"It can't be my little friend Rick on his moped," I said, "because we broke up."

"It's not little Rick, and it's not a moped," my mother said. "*This* is a grown man. And on a *motorcycle*, Rachel!" She said the word *motorcycle* as if she really meant *rattlesnake*.

"Really?" I jumped up. My heart was racing. I knew who it had to be.

Jason was revving up at the curb. He did sort of look sinister, something like a Hell's Angel out there, with his black boots and his helmet on. He looked bigger and meaner than he'd ever looked at The Bargain Buggy. I thought again: How little you could tell from a person's appearance about the condition of his soul.

Apparently my mother had sent out urgent signals to the family, because Franny came rushing down the front hall in her bare feet and peered out the front window.

"Is that *yours*, little sister?" she asked me with definite respect in her voice. "He's magnificent."

"I thought you had given up on men," I reminded her.

"Sometimes I just have a visceral response, I can't help it," she said.

"He's the Buddhist I told you about — the one that isn't available for ordinary love. So don't let your imagination carry you too far."

Erica came hurrying down the hall with my father.

"What's going on?" Erica asked. She had been sewing lace on a wedding garter, and she carried it with her — all lacy and blue — with a needle sticking out of it.

"Watch out with that thing!" my father said, shielding his face. "And what's everyone looking at?" He, too, began peering out the window.

"Rachel has a visitor," my mother said, coming up behind him, as if she hadn't just told everyone. "Would you *look* at him!"

"He doesn't look like your type, Rachel," my father said. "I doubt that he's Jewish."

"Don't generalize, Dad," Franny warned him. "That's the first blow to getting the wedge of bigotry in the door — it's only a small step from 'Jews don't ride motorcycles' to 'Jews don't belong in this town.' "

"You overreact to everything, Franny," Dad said.

"It's her mono," Mom said. "She's not herself."

"It's my *motto*," Franny said. "To overreact."

I let myself out the door, with my family watching from the window, and went to talk to Jason.

"Hi, Rachel."

"How did you ever *find* me?" I asked.

"Katya. You didn't come to The Bargain Buggy," he said, "but Katya was there filling up her bag, and she told me where you lived."

"Filling up her bag! Don't tell me they had another Stuff-Your-Bag day! Don't tell me I missed it!"

"Yup — and they had lots of nice black clothes," Jason said, with a teasing smile.

"Well, maybe I have enough black clothes," I said. "The hotter the summer gets, the more I feel I'm boiling alive in oil."

"I saw a nice white cotton jumpsuit over there," Jason said. "White would reflect the sun right off you. They just hung it up on the Designer Rack."

"I'm not *that* tired of black," I told him. "A person can't change commitments that easily. You should know that."

Then, for the sake of my family, I went close to the motorcycle and placed my fingers on the hand grip. With my other hand, I stroked Jason's helmet. "Speaking of hot, you must be melting under there."

"It's not bad," he said. "There's a breeze when you go fast. Want to go for a ride?"

"Sure," I said. I couldn't believe I'd said it. I didn't really *want* to go for a ride. I didn't *want* an interruption in my plans. I wanted to work in my

133

darkroom and finish making an enlargement of the devil chaser. I had cropped it so that the center of the picture was now the devil's piercing eyes. I was going to bring up the contrast dark and menacing. Then I was going to send it to the amateur photo contest sponsored by the newspaper.

But I didn't stick to my plan. No, possibly because I was only human, and because my mother, my father, and my sisters were watching, I tossed a leg over the seat behind Jason and hopped on.

"Uh-oh," Jason said. "I didn't bring my other helmet for you. Maybe we'd better not."

"I'll chance it. We can just go around the block. This is a quiet neighborhood; just don't go too fast."

"Well, take my helmet then. My skull is harder than yours."

I thought he looked gallant, the way he pulled his helmet off his head and handed it back to me. I placed it on my head. Then I wrapped my arms around Jason's waist and laid my helmeted head against his back. I pictured all the nosy noses pressed against the window of my house, all those nosy eyes watching us.

"Ready? Hang on, then!" Jason said. We *varoomed* off.

"Just don't head up the mountain!" I shouted. "I can't deal with seaweed again."

"Didn't you like it?" he called back in astonishment. Even in the wind, with the roar of the motor between us, he sounded disappointed in me. Everyone was disappointed in me.

Even old Mrs. Crutcheon, who we passed, recognized me, and her mouth fell open in disappointment. I could see her thinking: *Little Rachel Kaminsky gone bad. What a pity.*

"Hey, look, there comes Katya," Jason called over his shoulder to me. Katya was biking up the street; she was almost at her house. A big paper bag was stuck in a plastic tote hanging over her handlebar. Jason slowed down and pulled up at the curb just as she got there.

"Get some great bargains?" he called to her.

"Terrific," she said. "Rachel — is that you under there?"

"The one and only," I said.

"You should have come with me. I saw this great gorilla costume. Black! You would have flipped."

"Yeah," I said, "maybe I could have worn it to Erica's wedding. I'm looking for something original, something my mother would like."

Just then, the front door of Katya's house opened and Karl peered out. He, too, seemed astonished to see me slung over the back of a motorcycle, leaning against some guy. He squinted as if he weren't sure it was me. He shaded his eyes. He came down the steps toward the curb.

"Hey," he said to Katya. "That's not Rachel, is it? Not that same, serious girl who likes to bake *challah* and dance slow dances."

Jason twisted around on his seat. "Who's that?" he asked.

"Oh, that's just Katya's brother."

"You went dancing with him?"

"No, no!" I said. "I was baking bread with him. We only danced together by accident."

"Well, that certainly explains it," Jason whispered. He actually sounded hurt. "I wouldn't have expected that of you."

"Expected *what*?" I whispered back. "You hardly know me, everyone hardly knows me, and everyone expects something of me! Everyone is disappointed in me! What's wrong with everyone?!"

"Hey, what's going on with *you*?" Jason said. "You seem right on the edge."

Karl was standing right next to us by then. He said, "Why don't you come on in, Rachel? I have some great tangos we could try out."

The two men stared at each other.

Jason said, finally, "Want me to give you a ride home?"

I thought of my parents and sisters peering out the window, waiting for me to return.

"No thanks," I said. "I think I'll just sit here in the middle of the sidewalk and think about life for a while. You just all go on about your business. Go on. Go. Good-bye!" I shooed them away, like flies, or mosquitoes.

Maybe, because of the way I had said it, they decided to take me seriously. It amazed me that no one tried to dissuade me. Not Karl nor Katya, who just turned around and went into their house; not Jason, who shrugged, waved good-bye, and roared off on his bike.

Not even my parents, who — when I finally wandered home — didn't say a word when I came in the door. Even Franny and Erica kept their dis-

136

tance, as if I had just shown signs of a dangerous, contagious disease spread by a method they didn't quite understand.

I thought I might actually be in the terminal stages of a very fast-acting, fatal condition. I decided I had symptoms of heart failure, depression, and insanity. I went into the backyard and grabbed Itzhak and cuddled him against me. He always knew when I was sad and always did the right thing. He rubbed his whiskers against my cheek and tried to bite me very gently. His golden fur shone in the sunlight. Something about the way he held himself reminded me of a sphinx in Egypt. Maybe he had been a pharaoh in an earlier life — in any case, he had more dignity than any human being I knew.

Why did I feel this *rotten*? All week I had thought about the bride, Yeheuda, and how simple her life would be from now on. Everything was planned out — the way she would live, under what rules, how she would raise her children, how she would behave in the community. It seemed she had only to make that one decision, to marry Shlomo, and the rest fell into place. At some point she had to assume, of course, that he would sign the writ of marriage, which, luckily, he had.

All week this thought had nagged at me: *If I married Avram, my worries would be over. My father would be overjoyed.* (Avram would never ride a motorcycle!) *We would go and live in Israel and devote our lives to God.*

Then I wouldn't have to worry about senior year or The Mountainside School or applying to college or growing up or figuring out how to live or who to be. What a simple solution — get married and shift into automatic for the rest of my life.

But how could I marry Avram? Handsome as he was, he held stern opinions on too many things. He was too *righteous*. He seemed to think he "knew it all," and I knew — from being alive only sixteen years — that no one could know it all, and if they thought they did, they were wrong.

So there was no way I could take the easy way out. I couldn't marry Avram and have my life all laid out for me. Not that he had asked.

Should I marry Jason? Not that he had asked, either. But marriage was on my mind, what with Erica running around with her lace garter with its blue ribbon! Would I want to marry Jason and follow the ways of Zen? That wouldn't be an *easy* way out — achieving *satori* was hard! And Jason wasn't doing so well in his quest, I could tell. He still desired things. He certainly adored his bike, and I was pretty sure he was attracted to me. Well, that was good. I was attracted to him, too. But I didn't consider it a problem, and he did. I *wanted* to desire things. A boyfriend and a career didn't seem items too outrageous for me to have on my list of desires. But Jason wanted me not to have any list at all. And that was just as manipulative as Avram not wanting me to like certain kinds of people.

I liked *lots* of people. I also thought people were often incredibly stupid. Sometimes, though this was rare, I even loved everyone in the whole world. I just didn't like to be told who not to like or what not to desire. I liked Avram and Karl and Jason, as different as they were from each other. At various times I had imagined I could be in love with any or all of them. Was I boy crazy?

Boy crazy was what my grandmother used to say of a girlhood friend of hers. "That Rozzie, she was boy crazy. She had five boyfriends at once!"

Well, did I have three boyfriends? Could I count Karl and Jason and Avram as boyfriends? Karl had kissed me, but Jason had taken me up the mountain, and hanging on to him on the bike was in some ways more thrilling than the kiss. Avram, on the other hand, hadn't ever touched me, not really, but he had read to me from the *Song of Solomon*. Each one of those things had valence.

Like in chemistry, certain elements had what they called "valence" — *Valence is the force that determines with how many atoms of an element an atom of another element will combine.*

I felt a different valence toward Karl than I did toward Jason, and still a different one toward Avram. The trouble was: We weren't atoms, we were people.

I really liked Karl best — his humor, his easygoing nature, was wonderful. But the fact did trouble me, despite myself, that he was *German*. And it wasn't Avram I was worried about — it was my father. He, too, had this weird idea that you shouldn't marry Mexicans or Frenchmen or Canadians. How could a girl marry a country, anyway?

I tried to remember my instructions to myself: *Try to please everyone and you please no one. You can't please all of the people all of the time.*

So what should a person do?

Itzhak licked my face and then bit me gently.

Please yourself, Rachel, he told me in cat language. *That's who you have to live with.*

You're a wise old fellow, I meowed back to him. *That's the secret. I have to consider others, but in the end I have to please myself.*

Twenty

A long loaf of French bread with a blue baby bonnet tied around one end was left in a basket on our front steps the next morning. I found it when I opened the front door to let Itzhak and Basil outside.

For a second I thought someone had left a baby on our doorstep! My heart was thudding as I bent down and read the note pinned to the bonnet: *Warm me up and try me!* read the note.

I had to laugh. I called Katya's number, and when Karl got on, I was still laughing.

"Thank you," I said. "I love it."

"I deliver," Karl said. "Tomorrow look for muffins, the next day croissants, the next day a *sachertorte.*"

"You're sweet," I said.

"No, you've got it backward," he said. "You're the sweet one. Listen — I'm sorry about yesterday. I just was surprised to see you with that guy in black leather. I guess it's really none of my business."

"That's okay," I said. "He's just a friend I met in The Bargain Buggy. Katya was with me. You can ask her — I have all kinds of weird friends."

"Like me?"

"You might say so."

"Would you like to go to the movies tonight? They have *The Rocky Horror Picture Show* at the Rialto."

"I don't think so, Karl. But thanks."

"Is it my body odor, or what?"

I laughed. "No, I like your odor. You sort of smell like vanilla beans."

"That's the nicest compliment I ever got in my life. So why can't we go to the movies later? If you like vanilla, I'll shampoo with it. I'll shave with it. I'll wear vanilla bean earrings. Nothing is too much to please you!"

I heard myself laugh again.

"You have a splendid laugh, Rachel," Karl said.

In spite of myself, I had to laugh again. I'd never thought about how nice laughter sounded.

"I really can't go, Karl. My sister Erica is having a bridal shower this afternoon. I have to be there. And tonight we have to do more wedding stuff. Address invitations. I promised I would help."

"Do I get invited?"

"Well, sure, if you want to come."

"If you'll be there, I want to come. I love weddings. You should see the wedding cakes I've made at bakers' college. Did you ever see one with eight tiers? Only a master baker can do eight tiers, Rachel. Even in the circus, you never saw such a balancing act!"

"I can believe it," I said.

"So marry me. We'll get our cake at a discount. For you I'll make it ten tiers."

"You're silly," I said.

"Better silly than serious," he told me. "Life is serious enough. So marry me. At least think it over. Another year of bakers' college, and then we can dance the nights away."

"Thanks, Karl. I'm not quite ready to get married."

"I'll throw in a dozen bagels, free."

"You're sweet, Karl. Good-bye."

At The Pink Onion we were served salsa and blue corn chips while Erica giggled and opened her presents. She looked radiant — that's the only word that fit — with a red rose pinned in her hair, and her lipstick the same deep red, a perfect match. I'd never quite noticed before that she wore her hair in the same style as Mom's — parted on the side and very businesslike.

Franny, wearing a purple T-shirt and blue jeans (my mother wouldn't "allow" her to wear her purple shorts — " They are just not *appropriate* for a luncheon, Franny!") sat between me and our

143

mother at one end of the long table, while Erica had the seat of honor at the head of the table, flanked by all her girlfriends.

"Ooh, Ruth, you naughty girl," Erica giggled, as she unfolded something from a box. It was a pink lace teddy, covered with bows and frills.

"You're the one who can be naughty in that," her friend Ruth giggled back, and then all Erica's friends dissolved into laughter.

Beside me, Franny groaned. My mother looked embarrassed. In fact, she looked extremely uncomfortable. I knew my mother slept in a flannel nightgown in the winter, and in a plain cotton nightgown in the summer. I guess it wasn't easy for her to imagine her little Erica slinking around in a lacy teddy. It was even hard for me to picture — mainly because I also saw Harlan in the scene, with his round cheery face and his fuzzy head of hair. Neither one of them seemed cut out for seduction and passion — but who could know about anyone's inner life? I probably looked perfectly dull to others, myself — but I knew, when the time was right, I would adore being seductive and passionate. Only, of course, if the right man were part of my life.

Men! I pictured myself in a lace teddy, waltzing around the room while Avram watched me, frowning. No, indeed, that would *not* work. He'd be studying the Talmud, and my dancing would horrify him.

Well, while I was going through the men in my life, what about Jason? No, I didn't think so. If

Jason didn't want to allow himself "desire" — what was the point of my even trying to tantalize him with a bit of pink lace? On our honeymoon, I'd be trying to flag him down with my lacy teddy, and he'd be reading *The Way of Zen*!

And finally: Karl. Well, the rhythm of my heart told me I was getting warm. Karl! With him I could imagine being seductive in lace or silly in burlap. With him, my imagination knew no boundaries. He wasn't judgmental; he wasn't disapproving. He could let a person *BE*. In my imaginings, I could do anything wild or silly, say any thought that came to my mind. He'd be there, smiling and listening. And swirling in the air all around us would be the sweet, reassuring smell of bread baking, and the promise of nourishment and goodness.

Ah, yes — Karl seemed a real possibility. But Karl was going back to school in Chicago in another month. Karl was going to bake wedding cakes for hundreds of weddings. If I married Karl, we'd have a dozen blond, blue-eyed children. What would happen to my dark Jewish curls? Did babies ever come out half-and-half, like those cookies from my childhood, with dark chocolate icing on one half, white vanilla icing on the other?

What if in another few years — say after I was done with college — I met Karl and still felt the same way I did now? Even if he *was* German! Even if his ancestors and mine had been at war? Well, I simply would not allow that to enter into it. What counted (how well I was learning this lesson) was the *individual*. Maybe in the future I could prove to my family that a person's character was the only measure of worth. Not any line of descent, or religion, or genetic traits.

Erica was squealing and shrieking, holding up the next present, a set of matching pot holders. Six Mexican waiters, singing "Congratulations to you" to the tune of "Happy Birthday," gathered around Erica and presented her with a giant tostada, brimming with refried beans and shredded lettuce and guacamole and sour cream with an olive on top. Stuck knee-deep in the glob of guacamole was a little plastic bride and groom.

"Hang on, Franny," I told my sister. "Don't throw up. It's just part of the ritual."

"I can't take it," she whispered to me. "All this ecstasy! Do these girls think married couples really live *happily ever after* without ever having to give up anything or try hard at anything? Do they really think the moment you get engaged is the moment you can shut off your brain?"

"Don't you wish you could shut off your brain sometimes, Franny? Don't you? Don't you wish life weren't such a struggle?"

"It's not a struggle for *me*," Franny said. "I have mono — so that lets me off the hook for now."

"But you won't have mono forever. In the fall you'll go back to school, and you'll have to major in something, and then you'll have to graduate, and then you'll have to decide what job to take, and what man to marry — "

"Don't say that word!" Franny grabbed a blue corn chip and crushed it between her teeth.

Twenty-one

One day in the middle of August when I came home from camp, I found the letter waiting:

Dear Ms. Kaminsky —

The Admission Committee of The Mountainside School is pleased to inform you that you have been admitted as a student for the coming school year. We are also pleased to offer you a full scholarship. You will soon be receiving a detailed medical form, which must be returned to us, as well as a list of equipment you may wish to begin gathering before the fall term.

Congratulations on your outstanding school record, and on your future promise, on which your admission was based. We look forward to having you join The Mountainside School.

Sincerely yours,

Richard Babcock,
Headmaster

I grabbed the devil chaser and ran up and down the halls of my house, bouncing the stick and smashing the cymbals on the devil's head together.

"Yahoo!" I yelled. "Yippee! Hooray!"

"Rachel, what's wrong? Are you having a fit, Rachel?" Dad came running after me down the hall. "What's wrong?"

"I'm free!" I yelled. "No more pencils, no more books, no more teacher's dirty looks!"

"What are you talking about?"

"I'm accepted! I get to live on the mountain! I get to sleep under the stars."

"What *are* you talking about?"

I held the letter out to my father. "Remember, Daddy? You and Mom had to sign my application? You remember I told you about the school where you spend senior year on a bus?"

He read the letter with his brow furrowed. I realized from his surprised look that he hadn't taken seriously the possibility that I would be accepted.

148

"They gave me a full scholarship, Daddy! See? All those years with my birds weren't wasted after all!"

"But, Rachel," my father said firmly, "that's all well and good, but who is going to feed your birds while you're away?"

"I've been thinking about letting my birds go free, Daddy. In fact, I was thinking of doing it this afternoon."

"Let them go free? I thought some of those birds were quite expensive. Maybe you could sell them."

"But that isn't the point, Daddy. I think they'd be happier out in nature, with real birds. I'm pretty sure they would survive on their own. There's lots of natural food around, and I might even hang out a feeder, if you or Mom would keep it filled."

"Oh, Rachel," my father said. "Your mother and I will be all alone next year. Franny will go back to Berkeley, and Erica will be married, and you, our little baby, you'll be . . ."

"I'll be photographing the great American countryside. I may even turn out to be another Ansel Adams. You'll be so proud of me."

"But I don't know if we're ready to let you go, Rachel." My father waved the letter at me. It seemed to shake in his hands. "We didn't think we'd have an . . . empty nest . . . this soon."

Was my father, always so controlled, actually feeling sad? I realized, maybe for the first time, that he was a man with feelings. And he was getting old.

I went to him and threw my arms around him.

"Oh, Daddy," I said. "I really wanted to go to

149

this school so badly, and now I have the chance. Of course I'll miss you and Mom. Of course I'll be homesick. But I do have to grow up sometime, don't I?"

"Do you?" he said.

"You know I do," I said. I hugged him again. "Daddy, would you come with me while I set my birds free? It's kind of scary for me to do it by myself. I'd like you to be with me."

He didn't refuse, so I led him out the door and around to the side of the house. We surprised a wild parrot who was pecking at seed that had fallen on the ground around the edges of the aviary. I often heard the wild parrots screeching raucously in the early morning, as they flew in pairs across the sky, but I had never seen one up close. This one was brilliantly colored, his plumage a gaudy arrangement of red, green, and yellow feathers. He had a powerful gray beak, and seemed confident and independent, cracking the large sunflower seeds and making little curious dips with his head as he watched us.

My own birds inside the aviary were watching him with their dark, intense eyes. I counted eight birds now — my widowed finch, my cockatiel, the four mourning doves, and my pair of quails.

"Good-bye, children," I said, opening wide the door of the aviary.

At first, none of my birds made a move. Their eyes darted from me to my father to the parrot, who was still boldly pecking at seed. Then the finch took flight. He simply zoomed through the open door, made a single loop, and soared away. I watched him turn into a little dot against the blue sky and then disappear. My heart turned over. Then the first of the doves flew out and landed on top of the aviary. The other three followed, and there they were, free, but still at home.

"Maybe they don't want you to watch," my father said, putting his arm around me. "Why don't you come inside and let them go at their own speed?"

"You never let *me* go at my own speed."

"What do you mean?"

"In the car," I said. "You always want me to slow down."

"You can go at your own speed whenever you want to," my father said. "It's time, Rachel."

I kissed him. He was really sweet. I knew that letting me go wasn't easy for him.

Suddenly I was aware of a fluttering of wings, and two mourning doves flew away. In a flash of feathers, the other two followed.

The quails, not the brightest of my birds, were still looking around in the dirt inside the aviary.

"Give them time," my father said. "All creatures aren't the same. They come to you in many different forms. And they take off in different ways."

"Like me and Franny and Erica, right?" I said.

"Right," he said. "All different . . . and all ours."

Twenty-two

At our farewell party on the last day of camp, the kids were playing pin the *yarmulke* on the man. I had invited Katya to stop by for some *hamentachen* the kids had baked under my direction the day before. (The prune-filled, three-pointed delicacies hadn't come out too perfect, but we figured it didn't matter — the evil Hamen's hat-cookies didn't have to be perfect to make their point. If they were burned on the bottom, so much the better!)

Because camp was getting out early today, Katya and I were planning to go over to The Bargain Buggy to look for something interesting to wear to Erica's wedding.

I had three wedding invitations in my pocket —
one for Avram (just to be polite since he had asked
me to a wedding of *his* relative — but I knew he
wouldn't come to Erica's non-Jewish event); one
for Katya, Karl, and their parents, and one I
planned to leave with the nice lady who worked
at The Bargain Buggy to give to Jason, just in case
he showed up there in the coming week. I would
tell her: "Please give this to the tall guy who rides
the motorcycle," and she'd know in a second who
I meant.

"So *this* is where you worked all summer," Katya said, looking around the crafts room. "So
where's the interesting guy you told me about? The
one who's going to be a rabbi?"

"That's him, over there, talking to the kid dripping ice cream all over his tennis shoes."

"The one with the beard? Hey, he's *cute*."

"You think every guy is cute."

"That's not true. I only told you that about Jason," Katya said. "But Jason's not just cute, he's
gorgeous."

"Do you think your brother, Karl, is cute?"

"My *brother*. Why would I even *think* of my
brother as anything but a pest?"

"He's a guy," I suggested. "He's good-looking."

"Hey, don't tell me you have a thing for my
brother, Karl!"

"He's very likeable," I said. "He's sweet."

"You can't be talking about the lunatic who's
always putting stale bagels under my sheets, are
you?"

"I like his sense of humor," I said.

153

"You can have it," Katya said. "You can have *him*. But hey — do I get to meet the cute rabbi or not?"

"He's not a rabbi yet," I cautioned her.

"I think a beard is a very sexy thing on a guy," Katya confided in me. "Let's go meet him."

She tugged on my arm and half-dragged me across the room toward Avram.

"Hello, Rachel," he said. His voice had no special tone of acknowledgment in it — not a tinge of regret that it was the end of camp, not that it was the last day he might see me for a long time, or maybe forever. He was carrying his black looseleaf notebook under his arm.

I pulled the invitation from my pocket. "Just in case you're interested in observing a non-orthodox wedding, Avram — my sister's getting married this weekend. If you'd like to come, we'd love to have you."

"Oh, yes. I see, thank you," he said, staring at the envelope.

"It's not obligatory — you don't *have* to attend," I said. "It's only a suggestion."

"Well — " He looked as if he were trying to think of an extremely good reason why he couldn't possibly come.

"Don't worry about it," I said. "If you're free and you feel like dropping up the mountain, that's fine. And if not — that's fine, too. I know this kind of ceremony will seem very modern to you since the bride has a choice in this marriage, not only the groom."

I could see from his expression that he wasn't

going to discuss two thousand years of Jewish tradition with me, or defend Shlomo's position. Something about his look at me, the way he dismissed all the things I felt were important, made something go *ding* in my brain.

"Oh, just one second, Avram," I said, pulling Katya forward by the arm. "I'd like you to meet my cousin from Israel."

"Your cousin from Israel?" Katya croaked.

"She's so proud to be from Israel," I said to Avram. "She likes everyone to know it."

"From Israel?" Katya choked again.

"She's in the army there, too," I added, because it seemed like a good idea.

Avram turned to look at Katya with admiration in his eyes. "You have such fair skin and hair for an Israeli," he said. But then he seemed to realize that he shouldn't be taking notice of those things, so he said, "What part of Israel?"

"Oh, near the Dead Sea," I answered quickly for her. "Or is it the Red Sea? I forget."

"Hey!" Katya interrupted. "I — " But I poked her and she closed her mouth.

"And what is your name?" Avram asked Katya.

"Her name is Shoshana."

Katya's eyebrows shot up. I poked her again. "She doesn't speak much English, Avram," I warned him. "But she does understand it just fine."

"How nice," he said. "Tell me, Shoshana, would you like to try some of our *hamentachen*?"

"Sure," Katya answered.

Avram walked over to the long table on which we had set out our punch bowl and our party food.

He began piling some *hamentachen* on a paper plate.

"What are you *doing*?" Katya asked me. "Why am I suddenly your *cousin? From Israel?*"

"Just play along with me, okay? I had a sudden inspiration," I explained. "This is sort of a joke on Avram. He thinks you're his natural enemy, Katya. I want to show him he's wrong. So you don't even have to talk — just smile and look pretty and don't worry."

Avram returned with the food and offered the plate to Katya. He began to tell her how much he loved Israel, how he hoped to go and live there someday. Maybe he could even visit her there. He was just starting to tell her how he had had one of his three bar mitzvahs there. I heard some of my campers start to fight, so I excused myself and went over to the table where I insisted that Danny remove his finger puppet from the punch bowl!

When I came back to where Avram and Katya were standing, I heard Avram reciting something and saw Katya nodding her head:

> *"How beautiful are thy steps in sandals.*
> *O prince's daughter*
> *The roundings of thy thighs are like*
> *the links of a chain . . .*
> *Thy navel is like a round goblet . . .*
> *Thy two breasts are like two fawns*
> *That are twins of a gazelle . . ."*

"Isn't that magnificent?" he said to Katya.

"Avram likes to do a run-through of the *Song of*

Solomon to all the new girls he meets," I said. "I remember how he read it to me. I guess it's a good icebreaker."

"You *know* it's a beautiful poem, Rachel," Avram said in self-defense. "But your cousin doesn't seem to be familiar with it."

"Oh, God!" Katya burst out. "I can't keep a straight face another second! I'm cracking up! I'm not really her cousin, Avram," Katya confessed. "She's just teasing you."

"You're not her cousin? Not from Israel?"

"I'm just her friend. My name is Katya Ohlendorf. I live on Rachel's street. She's just playing some kind of joke on you."

Avram threw me a look heavier than the Ten Commandment tablets.

"So this is your *friend*," he said, and we both knew exactly which friend he meant. My *German* friend. But I had made my point. He had been attracted to Katya because she was so pretty and bright. Before he knew her origins, he had been willing to try to impress her and befriend her. I could even imagine that he might have become interested in her!

"I don't see there was a need for that, Rachel."

"Just a little joke, Avram," I said. "No harm meant."

"Well," he said, looking unsettled. "Will you ladies excuse me now? I have to attend to many things on this last day." We watched him walk off. As he passed the wastepaper basket, I saw him pause and drop Erica's wedding invitation into it.

"Well, he would have been a party pooper, anyway," I said.

The big black motorcycle was parked at the curb of The Bargain Buggy.

"Oh, no," I said. "I thought he only came on Saturdays."

"Don't you want to see him?"

"I'm giving up men," I told her. "I don't want to see *any*one. I have to practice for next year when I go off to the school on the mountain. *No pairing off* — that's their primary rule. What a relief that's going to be. It'll give me a chance to think about other things for a change."

"I think we women are biologically programmed to think about men," Katya says. "I saw a program on TV that proved that at certain ages our hormones cause us to act certain ways."

"That's probably why my mother doesn't wear lace teddies to bed," I said. "Her hormones don't suggest it to her. Besides, she has all the biological results she can handle."

I kept talking, hesitating to go into the thrift shop. My heart was skipping beats. I decided I was biologically programmed to get excited at the sight of the motorcycle. Katya seemed to be feeling the same thing.

"Maybe he'll give me a ride," Katya said. "I can tell him I'm your cousin from Israel, and I never, ever saw a motorcycle in my life. I'll tell him we only get to ride on tanks in Israel."

"Never mind," I told her. "Just never mind."

"I *still* don't know why you told your rabbi friend

that I was your cousin from Israel."

"It was just a private little joke," I told Katya. "He knows why. Don't worry about it." There was no way I could explain this to Katya. She didn't even *know* she was German, not in any cultural sense, just as she had never thought, I was sure, about the fact that I was *Jewish*. I didn't want to ruin her innocence.

"Let's take the plunge," Katya said. She took my arm and pulled me into The Bargain Buggy.

I didn't see Jason in his usual armchair, and at first I thought we might have been mistaken to think he was there. But then I saw him bending over the luggage bin. When he straightened up, holding an old suitcase, he saw us.

"Rachel!" he said. His blue eyes lit up. And he gave me his smile; I had to respond. It was involuntary, probably hormonal. Katya had said so. I smiled back.

"I'm glad I found you here," I said. "I was going to drop off this invitation to my sister's wedding and ask Faith to give it to you the next time she saw you."

At the sound of her name, the woman at the front desk looked up and grinned at us from under her wig of red curls.

Jason took the invitation from me and opened it.

"Hmm," he said. "This is great. I love this little map right on the invitation — of how to get to Red Pine Ranger Station and then go up the trail to the clearing. What a great idea to get married on the mountain."

"My sister and her boyfriend are going to recite poetry to each other under God's blue sky," I said. "So will you come?"

"Let's see — it's in a week. I guess I could put off leaving till then."

"Leaving? For where?" I asked.

Katya echoed my words. "For where?" she said, disappointment heavy in her voice.

Jason indicated the suitcase he had set down at his feet. It was one of those old, elegant leather suitcases with someone's initials embossed in gold on it. The leather was cracked, but it still looked very handsome.

"I'm setting off to see the world," Jason said. "I've been in one place long enough."

"Not long enough for me," Katya said. I poked her. It seemed to me that Katya had to be poked more often these days than ever before in our long relationship. "Will you come back?"

"Oh, sure, maybe in a year or so. I have some friends out in Santa Fe, and I'm going to stay with them for a while. One is an artist — he does sand sculptures. And his wife is a painter." He smiled at me. "But hey, that's great about your sister's wedding. I'll certainly try to come. I love weddings — as long as they aren't mine."

Katya and I looked at each other.

"It'll be fun riding my bike up those mountain roads," Jason said. "I haven't been up a mountain since I took you to the Zen Center," he told me.

"Maybe you'd like me to ride with you," Katya suggested.

"*Never mind*, Katya," I reminded her. "I thought you and Karl were driving up with your folks."

"Oh, yeah, I forgot."

"Well," Jason said. "Excuse me while I hunt up a few more things here. I don't own much in the way of long underwear, and my friend says it gets pretty cold in his tent sometimes."

"His *tent*?"

"He lives in a tent," Jason said. "But that's okay. It's a big Indian tepee. He's into Indian art. So he likes to live like the Indians used to live." Jason walked off and started looking on the long-underwear table.

I went over to the black-shirt rack, but my heart wasn't in it. They all looked exactly alike: black. I had a whole closet full of stuff like this.

I wandered along the aisles, running my hands over the racks of colorful clothing. I stopped at the red rack. Hanging on it were dresses in various combinations of red: one had red and white polka dots, one had red stripes, one had a pattern of red, white, and blue flags. But what was this one, glittering and shining? It was a red gauze dress shot through with gold thread, hemmed with gold spangles. A dress from India. I took it off the rack and held it up to my chin.

Faith, at the front desk, was watching me. "That's gorgeous, honey," she said. "You would look stunning in that. It's your color."

I put it quickly back on the rack as Jason came toward me. He had a paper bag in his hand, and he held it out to me.

"A good-bye present for you," he said. "I saw this, and I wanted you to have it. I think maybe you're ready for it."

"For me? Really? I opened the bag and pulled out a fleecy white cottony thing, soft as a cloud.

"For your next stage of discovery," Jason said to me. "What do you think?"

I was examining it, figuring out what it was — a two-piece sweatsuit, made of the softest, snowy-white, fleecy flannel-knit I had ever seen. It looked brand-new; it was, in fact, from the Designer Rack, since it had two little "Hang Ten" footprints on it.

"That's wonderful, Jason," I said. "I love it. Thank you very much. It's been a long, black summer."

"That's what I figured," he said. "We all have to move on. Maybe you can evolve into a warm, white winter."

He slid his newly acquired suitcase along the checkout table and ducked his head in farewell at Faith. He saluted to Katya and to me. Then we watched his tall figure go out the door. A moment later we heard the start-up roar of his motorcycle. Something in me expanded and then cracked in my chest. It was as if, for one second, I could feel a tiny part of my heart breaking.

Twenty-three

This is the way the world ought to be, I decided. *Flowers, music, earth, sky, wind . . . and love.*

The wedding party was on its way up the mountain: Car after car filled with guests, food, and gifts labored along the steep, winding road.

Franny and I were standing together beside the little watchtower at the ranger's station, looking below at the view of the valley and watching the caravan of guests arrive. Tall pine trees lined the mountainside, and the city lay below us, shrouded delicately in smog.

I was wearing my new red gauze dress! I had bought it at The Bargain Buggy, filled with doubt about breaking my long tradition. But this morning, seeing myself in the mirror, I decided I was happy with the risk I'd taken. I thought I looked like an Indian princess. Even now I gave a little spin, and the gold threads of my dress caught the sunlight and glittered around me like dancing butterflies.

At home this morning I had laid out on my bed my black T-shirt, leaving it there like the shell of a caterpillar. I had emerged down the hall — a fluttering, bright creature — to the absolute shock of my family.

Dad's mouth fell open, Mom gasped with pleasure, Erica told me I would be the prettiest thing on the mountaintop next to her, and Franny ran to lend me her red-and-gold dangling earrings. As she fastened them in my ears, she whispered to me, "What do you think? I might even wear a dress, myself, for a change. Even strong women are entitled to wear a dress once in a while, don't you think so? I might even shave my legs for this occasion!"

Now Franny stood beside me in a yellow cotton dress, looking frail and delicate. She had lost weight during her illness, and in some ways I thought I looked older than she did. And maybe even as beautiful. I don't know what it was — my eyes, or the way the earrings made me look grown up, or the way the dress fell gracefully around my hips, but I was impressed with myself. I felt all pumped up with emotion.

Just then Franny grabbed my arm. "That's him,

isn't it?'' We seemed to have heard it at the same moment — a distant buzz. And when we looked down upon the winding mountain road, we saw Jason's motorcycle approaching. With his dark helmet on, he looked like a little ant creeping up a steep hill. He glanced up as if he knew we were there, and we both waved at him.

At the big banquet table, Katya and Karl were fussing with putting together the tiers of the wedding cake. The Ohlendorfs were standing nearby, giving last-minute suggestions to Karl as he set up the pillars for each layer of the cake. Mrs. Ohlendorf had made little white, powdered-sugar *Pfeffernüsse* cookies to use as decorations around the rim of the bottom layer.

I hoped the cake would balance! At my urgent insistence, my mother had canceled her order to the Wedding Day Bakery and agreed to let Karl make his eight-tier wonder for the happy couple. He had even let me help him with the batter; the first thing we did was go to The Bargain Buggy and buy up every one of their old mixing bowls and baking pans. All week I had been at the Ohlendorfs, mixing and measuring and horsing around with Karl. We'd promised to write each other next year — as soon as I figured out what kind of address I would have at The Mountainside School bus-classroom. We kept it lighthearted, but we both agreed that we definitely wanted to keep in touch with one another.

* * *

At the ceremony, I stood with my parents and Franny and got all teary when Erica and Harlan took their vows under God's blue sky. Harlan sang the lyrics from The Shrunken Heads new album called *Commitment*, and Erica responded by singing, in harmony, the lyrics from one of their older songs, "Passion." At least the group had advanced to a three-syllable lyric ("Com-mit-ment"), which I thought showed a certain intellectual advancement.

Commitment and passion, not such a bad combination for a marriage. Later this afternoon, Harlan and Erica were going to sign some formal papers at City Hall, but this, as far as they were concerned, was the *real* thing. When their love songs to each other were finished, each lover took a handful of rose petals from my mother's crystal punch bowl and flung it into the air. Everyone cheered under the rain of flowers, and Erica and Harlan kissed each other for a long, wonderful time, and then the wedding ceremony was over!

Instantly, Harlan's friends who made up the Scottish dance group — six men dressed in kilts, and six women dressed in white dresses, each wearing a clan's tartan scarf draped around her neck — came forward over the weedy mountainside clearing to a good flat place for dancing. My father, dressed in a dark blue suit, turned on the portable tape player.

The men in their kilts, each with a little leather purse slung over his belly, looked awfully cute in their green plaid, pleated skirts. I glanced at

Franny, knowing it would amuse her to see men in skirts. Just behind Franny was my mother, dressed in blue organdy, sobbing happily. It was the first time I had really seen anyone cry with joy. She had been full of tears all day.

This morning my mother had announced at breakfast, as if we didn't know, "I'm giving away my eldest daughter today." She had cried then, as well. She looked at Franny and me, her remaining girls, and she said, "I pray for this lucky day to come for you children, as well."

Daddy, upset to see her in tears, went to comfort her. "Don't be sad. They'll come to see us, don't worry. And you and I — we'll have a second honeymoon; you'll see, we'll be happy," he assured her while we watched. "It's true all three of our girls will be gone next year and of course we'll miss them, but" — he swept his hand toward us as if, magically, we had already vanished from their sight — "then we'll be just like we used to be. Just Snookums and his little Boopsie."

Snookums! Boopsie! Erica and Franny and I had looked at one another and then burst into laughter as Dad and Mom hugged one another. I know I felt a great relief, and I think my sisters did, too, to know that our parents would still have each other after we were gone, and that they still loved each other.

Now the Scottish dance music brightened the air. The little group did a few traditional dances and then invited everyone to join in. The bride and groom stepped forward and did a little jig together.

Then my father invited my mother to dance. Katya began to dance all alone, looking quite beautiful and graceful.

"Oh, Rachel," Franny whispered to me, "we're really all growing up."

"It's all right," I assured her. "We're supposed to."

The music resonated off the hillsides, and the sun came down like bits of diamonds. I felt generous toward everyone because soon I was leaving them — and I loved them all. Even if they were bossy and full of advice for me, I knew they had done it with the best intentions. I knew they loved me and were doing the best they knew how to do. But most important of all, I was proud of myself for having taken a stand. I had figured out what I wanted, and I was going after it!

From the edges of my vision I saw them both at once, Jason and Karl, coming toward me. I knew it instantly, the way you know important things, with total certainty, that they were both going to ask me to dance.

They advanced from opposite directions, my friends, two handsome young men, smiling, their eyes on me, their hands extended toward me with hope and sweet invitation. I thought I would burst with happiness.

But instead I turned to Franny and offered her my arm. "May I have this dance?" I said to her.

"Indeed you may," she said.

Then the two of us wrapped our arms about one another and began to dance together, spinning and laughing under the tall trees and the vaulted sky.